# Spies

# &

# Sweethearts

## By Linda Shenton

## Matchett

*Spies & Sweethearts*

By Linda Shenton Matchett

Chapter One

Just because she was the eldest, did Cora have to criticize Emily's every decision? She was a high school French teacher, not a schoolgirl. Shaking her head, Emily climbed on the bike and pedaled away from the house. She'd exhausted her gas rations for the week, so using the car was out. Fortunately, the library wasn't far. She could finish preparing the end-of-year exams there.

Two of her students were already gone. Days after they turned eighteen, the boys talked the principal into letting them graduate early in order to enlist. Her heart constricted. Now, both were in training with the army air force and would soon be on their way overseas to fight the Germans. They spoke French impeccably, a skill better used in the ambassador ranks rather than on an airplane.

The warm air stroked Emily's cheeks as she rode. Squinting against the sun's glare, she huffed out a breath. At least the boys were doing something for the war effort. Her service with the American Women's Voluntary Services as a plane spotter and messenger wasn't exactly going to turn the tide against the Axis powers. Surely, there was something more she could do.

She braked in front of the sandstone building and wheeled her bike into an empty spot in one of the racks near the entrance of Trafalgar Public Library. A Carnegie library, it housed several hundred books thanks to the Scottish-American philanthropist. What would he think of the war?

"Emily!"

A broad grin on her face, Joan Boyer hurried toward Emily. Her floral dress danced around her leg, and her ponytail flounced. "Your mom said I'd find you here." Her smile faltered. "Are you okay? You look terrible."

"Gee, thanks. Glad I can count on you for support."

"What?"

Emily finger-combed her hair. "I'm sorry. I had another argument with Cora. Just because she's already been married and widowed, she thinks she knows what's good for everyone."

Joan linked her arm through Emily's. "Let's grab a seat in the memorial garden. You can tell me everything."

They sauntered to the wooden bench sheltered by a large, weeping cherry tree and surrounded by black-eyed Susans, and a rainbow of coneflowers and petunias nodding in the breeze.

"All right. What gives? You've been annoyed with Cora in the past, but you seem especially angry today."

"I am." Emily slumped against the seat. "True or not, it feels like neither she nor Doris take me seriously because I'm the youngest. That all I'm good enough for is teaching a bunch of kids. A few days ago, Cora commented that plane spotting night duty must be interfering with my job, and she didn't understand why I was still volunteering. Like I can't juggle multiple responsibilities. I'm almost twenty-six years old. I'm quite capable."

"Maybe she worries about you."

"Perhaps, but it doesn't seem like concern. It feels like criticism of my life." Emily fisted her hands. "This morning, I got a letter telling me I've been accepted into a new government program. I leave for training the day after school is out. She overheard me telling Mom about the job and quizzed me about it. When I told her I couldn't share specifics, she rolled her eyes and asked what the government needed with a schoolteacher."

"That's awful." Joan squeezed Emily's shoulder.

"The worst of it is that once she got started down that road, Mom followed…said I should rethink the opportunity…that I have a perfectly good job here at home, and my volunteer work is sufficient." She frowned. "Then Mom said I'm being selfish to go off on my own. It's bad enough I'm still living at home at my age, but for them to try to dictate my decisions is too much."

"What are you going to do?"

"Send a telegram accepting the position. I've got to live my own life no matter what they say." She blinked away tears forming in her eyes. "Do you think I'm being self-centered by going?"

"Absolutely not. Your parents are in perfect health, and Cora is living here, too. She can take care of any needs they might have." Joan leaned forward. "You really can't say much about the job? Not even a little?"

The tightness in Emily's chest eased, and she chuckled. "You always could make me feel better. I'm sorry for not telling you I applied, but I was skeptical I'd get selected. You should have seen the crowd. Anyway, I don't know a lot about the job. There is a new governmental department, and it needs people who are bilingual. The exam contained lots of translation exercises, especially with regard to colloquialisms and dialect for different regions in France and French-speaking countries."

"Now you know how your students feel."

"Absolutely, but that doesn't mean I'm going to go easy on them for the final." Emily rubbed her damp palms on her skirt. "I can't believe this will be my last year of teaching for a while…maybe forever. I'm a bit nervous about notifying the principal about leaving. The factories pay much higher than the schools, so Medford has had a lot of resignations. The school may have to combine classes next year."

"This war won't last forever. In fact, some say it will be over by Christmas. Surely you'll be back."

Emily shook her head. "I don't want to be a naysayer, but I doubt the war will be over by the end of the year. I think we're in this for the long haul."

"Can you at least tell me where you're going? I could come visit."

"I've forgotten the address, somewhere in Washington, DC, but that's not my final stop. I'll be transported with other new employees to the training facility where I'll stay for three months. I won't be able to send or receive letters while I'm there. And definitely no visitors."

Joan bolted upright. "That sounds intriguing, very secretive. If you're lucky, there will be a few dreamboats in the class."

"Romance is the last thing I need, Joan. Besides, guys our age are in the defense industry or armed forces. There won't be anyone to fall in love with."

---

Gerard Lucas resisted the urge to run a finger around the collar of his dress uniform to loosen the stifling piece of clothing. What he wouldn't give to be in a flannel shirt and pair of overalls. Out in the field, wind ruffling his hair, and acres of crops flourishing in the sunshine. Perhaps a beautiful woman by his side. And—

"Lieutenant Lucas, are you listening to me?"

Gerard wrenched his thoughts back to the present and snapped his heels together. "Sir, yes, sir."

"Insulting and then arguing with a higher ranking officer in front of his men and the local Brits is a serious offense. The only things keeping you out of the brig or a dishonorable discharge are this war and the fact you didn't take a poke at him. The country needs all the men we can get." Major Albert shook his head. "You're a bright guy, one who should be climbing the ranks rather than getting demoted every three months. You are lucky Major Quigley had you reduced to private."

"Sir, he didn't know what he was talking about—"

"I did not give you permission to speak, and therein lies your problem. Failure to respect the chain of command. You are to obey orders without question and to show respect to those ranked above you. You're arrogant and argumentative. More than a few officers have made that observation. Not a good combination, Lucas." The major dropped into the chair behind his desk. "You need to apologize to Major Quigley. In public. At the pub where the incident occurred."

"Yes, sir."

"Excellent. Now, the good news for everyone is that you are being transferred to an intelligence unit based out of Washington, DC. Apparently, your penchant for getting into trouble is a desirable trait to them."

Gerard's heart sped up. There'd been stories about guerrilla warfare and espionage, but he figured the information was rumor, like most of what he heard in between training exercises. Was he finally going to see the war up close? Or rather, behind the scenes?

Major Albert tossed him a set of papers then gestured to the vacant chair. "At ease, Soldier."

Dropping into the seat, Gerard tugged at his collar and sighed. The material still scratched his skin and threatened to suffocate him. He picked his orders and scanned the instructions. He had two days to prepare. To wait and wonder what was in store for him.

"As you can see, you leave the day after tomorrow. Unless you run into a hitch, you'll report for duty on Saturday. Try not to mess this up. It may be your last chance to remain a free man."

"Permission to speak candidly, sir?"

"I'd expect nothing less, Lucas."

"Why me?"

"Why you, what?"

"You must have recommended me, sir. Otherwise, how would they know about me?" Gerard studied the major. "So why did you put my name forward for consideration?"

"It appears I haven't underestimated your abilities. You're right. I did recommend you." Major Albert smirked. "This new department...they're calling it the Office of Strategic Services...a positively bureaucratic label, if you ask me, but maybe that's what they want everyone to think. Personally, from the bits and pieces I've been able to glean, it's more like the department of dirty tricks. Anyway, that sounded like something you'd be suited for. You know, swimming against the tide."

"I appreciate your faith in me, sir. I won't let you down."

"It's not me I'm worried about. Don't let yourself down, Lucas. You've got to come to terms with whatever's eating you. Yes, you don't suffer fools, and that's fine, but it's more than that. You're carting around a lot of anger. Maybe you know why. Maybe you don't. Either way, you need to channel those feelings or jettison them, because if you don't, you'll get yourself killed. Understood?"

"Yes, sir."

Major Albert steepled his fingers. "Quigley wanted to bring you up on charges, put you through a court-martial, but I talked him out of it."

"Thank you, sir."

"I'm not looking for gratitude. I'm telling you because this is your last chance. Not everyone is willing to accept your shenanigans. And despite the roguish nature of your new assignment, there will be some sort of hierarchy. Adhere to it, or you may not survive this war." He rose and extended his hand. "Good luck, son, and Godspeed."

They shook hands. Gerard put on his peaked wool cap, saluted, then pivoted and hurried from the room, a grin tugging at his lips. Finally, a chance to avenge his brother's death in the Atlantic at the hands of a German submarine wolfpack.

Chapter Two

Emily clutched her pocketbook in her lap and stared out the airplane window. The macadam glistened with rain that spattered the baggage handlers tossing suitcases into the hold. Her heart skittered with each bump that sounded from below. Surveying the other passengers, she nibbled her lower lip. Men in suits, many carrying briefcases, women in their Sunday best. Air hostesses adorned in navy-blue dresses and jaunty pillbox hats walked the aisle providing assistance and direction.

Minutes ticked past. The plane filled, yet the seat next to her remained vacant. Who would share the journey with her? Would it be an experienced traveler or a first timer like herself?

She opened her handbag and checked its contents for the umpteenth time. Lipstick, tickets, notification letter, notepad, pencil, and a pocket-sized New Testament from Joan who'd stopped by last night for a final hug.

Their conversation replayed in her mind, and she smiled. Always supportive, her friend brushed away Emily's concerns with jokes and laughs. Brazen to a fault, Joan made more than a few suggestions about the opportunity for Emily to meet men during her new venture.

"Everything all right, miss?"

Emily glanced at the stewardess whose name badge read ANN and nodded. "Yes, thank you. Just a tad nervous. I've never flown before."

The woman's face creased with a smile. "You're going to love it. The feeling of speed and freedom. The sky is gorgeous above the clouds, like swimming in a sea of whipped cream. I flew for the first time three years ago and decided then I wanted do it for a living. And here I am."

"Did you ever consider becoming a pilot?"

"Heavens, no. I'd much rather interact with the passengers than be stuck in the cockpit for hours on end." She patted her well-coifed hair. "So many people going to Washington, the airline has added four flights each day. Are you going down there to work?"

"Yes, but that's not my final destination. Once I complete my training, I'll receive an assignment. It's kind of exciting, yet nerve wracking not knowing where I'll serve. I'm usually organized with plans and lists, so having someone else take care of things is…well…"

Ann patted Emily's shoulder. "I understand. Sit back and relax. I'll take good care of you, and we'll be landing before you know it."

"Wait!" A muffled shout sounded outside the craft, and footsteps clattered. Seconds later, a tanned, sandy-haired man carrying a duffle bag appeared, his face red and perspiring. Out of breath, he sagged against the door, his ice-blue eyes searching the plane.

Averting her gaze, Emily studied her hands. Please don't sit here. Please don't sit here—

Waving, Ann pointed to the vacant seat next to Emily. "Sir, here's a spot, but you must hurry. We're about to close the doors and take off."

Emily's heart sank, and she looked up.

The man nodded, his mouth set in a thin slash. He clumped down the aisle, shoved his bag under the seat in front of him, and dropped next to her with a grunt. Strapping himself in, he crossed his arms and glared at her.

Her neck stiffened. It wasn't her fault he nearly missed the plane. Two could play his game. She looked down her nose at him, then turned and watched the activity through the tiny circular window.

Next to her the man shifted, sighing every time he moved. It was going to be a long flight. Better to focus on her destination, away from the irritated passenger who she'd never see again once they landed.

She tucked her hair behind her ears and settled into her seat then opened her purse, withdrawing the slim, leather-bound Bible. The tissue-paper pages rustled as she turned them. Delighted to see the Psalms were included in the volume, she found her favorite and began to read silently.

"O Lord, thou hast searched me, and known me. Thou knowest my downsitting and mine uprising, thou understandest my thought afar off. Thou compassest my path and my lying down, and art acquainted with all my ways."

The archaic language touched her heart, and the tightness in her chest eased. When would she learn to turn over her day to the Lord?

Always rushing to get where she was going or worried about the next thing. She smiled. He was in control.

"I don't remember anything funny in the Bible."

Her gaze shot to the man beside her. "I beg your pardon?"

"You're grinning as if you read something amusing. That's not the Bible I know."

"Then perhaps you haven't read it in full, because I know of several stories that are quite droll. But I'm smiling with joy, not entertainment." She cocked her head. "When was the last time you looked inside the Bible?"

A muscle in his jaw jumped, and he shrugged. "A while."

She tucked a finger between the pages and closed the Bible. A touchy subject apparently. "Why are you headed to Washington? I'm going for new job."

"How nice for you."

"You must be traveling on business. With the war on, no one is taking vacations. The whole country seems to be working day and night. Wouldn't you agree?"

"Sure. Look, are you going to talk the whole time we're in the air?"

Emily raised an eyebrow. "Not if you'd prefer silence, but I have one more question."

"Yes?"

"Are you always this rude to people you've only just met?"

Gerard's face heated. The woman had spunk; he'd give her that. And she was right. He'd allowed a poor start to the day to color his attitude, pouring disdain onto anyone close by. First, the cab he'd taken to the airport broke down, and the wait for a replacement was interminable. Then after finally arriving at the airport, a comedy of errors sent him to the wrong gate, not once, but twice. Sprinting the last hundred yards to the plane in dress shoes was an athletic feat Olympian Jim Thorpe would have been proud of. Now, he was being asked questions he couldn't answer.

He held out his hand. "I apologize. My morning did not have an auspicious beginning, and I've taken it out on you. I'm Gerard Lucas."

She flashed a smile and grasped his hand. "My name is Emily Strealer. Perhaps I'm at fault as well. I can be a chatterbox when nervous. This is my first time on an airplane." Dimples bracketed her mouth, and her eyes sparkled. Porcelain skin shone even in the dim light of the aircraft.

"You'll be fine. Technology has come a long way since the Wright Brothers."

"Are you a pilot?"

"Yes. I did some crop dusting in my younger days, so the air force seemed to be the right place to enlist. I didn't want to end up in the trenches. I've flown mostly Thunderbolts, but I managed to get my hands on a Mustang a couple of times. Now, that's a fast plane."

"I imagine being a fighter pilot is dangerous. You must be very brave."

He narrowed his eyes. How many times had some simpering gal hung on his arm, batted her eyelashes, and given him that line? This girl's tone seemed matter of fact. Maybe she didn't chase flyboys. "No braver than the next guy. We're all just doing what has to be done."

"As are we all."

"Do you have anyone in the service? Brother? A sweetheart?" Gerard held his breath. Had he offended her again? He had no right to ask about boyfriends.

She shook her head, and a shadow crossed her face. "I have two sisters. The eldest lost her husband at Pearl Harbor. And there's no one special in my life."

His thoughts tumbled. Why was he relieved she didn't have a beau? "I'm sorry about your brother-in-law. The nation lost a lot of good people that day."

A nod, then she nibbled her lower lip. His gaze shot to her mouth, small, tinted with light pink lipstick, and kissable. He almost reared back in the seat. Where had that idea come from? Yes, she was attractive, but he didn't usually go for redheads. Leggy blondes were more his type. Betty Grable or Gloria Graham. Either of them was the ticket.

"Good morning, ladies and gentlemen. This is your captain. We're cleared for takeoff and will be in the air shortly. Sit back and enjoy the ride. We'll try to avoid any bumps."

"Bumps? What bumps?" Miss Strealer's eyes bugged, and she gripped his arm.

Gerard patted her icy fingers. Where was the spirit he'd seen earlier? "He's kidding. Well, kind of. There's something called turbulence which happens when two masses of air moving at different speeds come together. The phenomena can cause the plane to rock a bit if we happen to fly through."

"Will it cause us to crash?"

"No. We'll be fine." Great, they got a pilot with a sense of humor. Gerard rolled his eyes. Probably some old codger left over from the last war. He pried off her hand, and placed it in her lap. "There is no need to worry."

The aircraft taxied down the tarmac and lifted to the sky. Gravity pushed him against his seat, and he closed his eyes. Takeoff was his favorite part of flying. Feeling the power then overcoming the pressure. Knowing he was in control. He'd miss being a pilot, but the new assignment promised greater challenges, more danger. Just what he needed.

The plane reached cruising altitude. He leaned toward his seat mate. "Now, that wasn't too bad, was it?"

A smile was back on her face, and her eyes glowed. "Exciting and fun. I don't understand the physics, but overcoming the pressure to get airborne was incredible. A sense of…I don't know…victory."

"My thoughts exactly. Now you know why I fly."

She pointed to the cotton-ball clouds outside the window. "You get a whole other perspective up here, don't you? By all appearances the clouds are cushioning us, but in reality, they are just masses of water. I don't think I'll look at them the same after this."

"Seems like you're getting bit by the flying bug." He grinned. Not nearly as annoying now that the woman wasn't quizzing him about God or war business; she was enjoyable to be around. Too bad a relationship wasn't in the cards at the moment. He might change his mind about what type of girl he stepped out with.

Hours passed. Nearing their destination, the aircraft began its descent.

Seconds later, the plane bucked, and Gerard's head whipped toward his lovely seat mate.

Miss Strealer gasped and gripped the arms of her chair, her face ashen.

The pair of stewardesses staggered in the aisle. Dishes rattled, and a woman in the back cried out.

Gerard rubbed his face. Apparently, the flight was not going to be a smooth one. "Are you okay?"

"Yes. I feel rather foolish reacting like this. My sisters would say my behavior is proving them right...that I should stay home where I belong." She spoke through clenched teeth.

"Nonsense. The first time I experienced turbulence, I almost lost my lunch."

She giggled. "I doubt that, but thanks for trying to make me feel better."

"What?" He widened his eyes in mock innocence. "You don't believe me?"

"No. I was warned about pilots. Always weaving stories in an effort to impress the girls." She smirked. "Although I guess claiming to get sick isn't exactly awe-inspiring."

The airplane touched down and raced down the tarmac before rumbling to a stop near the terminal.

In Gerard's peripheral vision, Miss Strealer hunched into her seat, eyes closed, and lips moving. Praying? Was she a believer or just a desperate flyer grasping at straws?

A bang sounded on the hull, and the stewardess opened the hatch, fresh air filling the cabin.

"We made it." He tapped her shoulder.

Miss Strealer's eyes popped open, and a tentative smile tugged at her mouth. "Yes, we did. Thanks again for being such a good sport. Babysitting a Nervous Nellie was not on your to-do list."

He chuckled, and she pinked as she stood. Stepping into the aisle, he gave her room to precede him out of the plane. They descended the steps, and she stumbled, falling against him. The floral scent of her shampoo invaded his senses as he wrapped his arm around her shoulder to steady her. She fit against his side perfectly. He gulped and released her as if burned.

Had she tripped intentionally? Was she being coy? He froze. Maybe she was a test, a part of his new assignment. Was he being watched? Now, who was being nervous?

## Chapter Three

A chilly wind lifted Emily's hair as she walked across the forty-acre campus. Unseasonably blustery, the temperature hovered just above frigid. She drew her coat closer and hunched into the collar. Two weeks had passed since her arrival at the training facility, located somewhere in Virginia. Or was it Pennsylvania? Everything was so secretive, students were given information on a "need to know" basis. Apparently, the instructors didn't think she needed to know much, including where she was.

The days were long and packed with lecture after lecture, the nights with memorization and homework. Her eyes burned from all the reading, and her brain ached from studying. College had been a lark by comparison.

She approached the small creek that ran through the property. Her roommate sat on its banks tossing stones into the water.

"Mind if I join you, Martha? I've got about twenty minutes before my next class and couldn't stand being inside one more minute."

Martha smiled and gestured to the ground beside her. "Me, too. I'm a farmer's daughter. My life before this was spent outdoors. Too much time between four walls isn't healthy." She shuddered. "How're you holding up?"

Emily shrugged. "I've always been a good student, voracious reader, and all that, but there are times I feel overwhelmed and wonder what I've gotten myself into. Am I smart enough to see this through?"

"I'm holding on to the fact that they wouldn't have selected us if they didn't think we could do the job."

Birds chirped overhead, and chipmunks chattered in the bushes. The river water gurgled and danced in the sunshine that warmed Emily's back.

She tucked her hair behind her ears. "That's true as far as getting into the program, but four people have already washed out, one of whom departed on the second day. This is a difficult course. Certainly the hardest thing I've ever done."

"I don't want to borrow trouble, but I think it's only going to get tougher. We haven't touched codes and ciphers yet or done any fieldwork. I may be strong, but I'm not sure I'm cut out for climbing trees or hiking over mountains."

"You're supposed to be making me feel better." Emily nudged Martha's shoulder.

Martha chuckled. "Right. Sorry." She skipped a rock across the water's surface. "Hey, did you like Mr. Smith's class? And by the way, we have too many professors named Smith and Jones. If they're going to practice all this cloak-and-dagger stuff, just assign letters. You know like Professor Q."

"Or Mr. X." Emily smoothed her slacks. "What did you think the job was going to be? I assumed they were hiring me for my ability to translate French. I don't see why I have to learn police procedures like how to search a house or conduct surveillance on a person."

"What about me? My claim to fame is animal husbandry and crop rotation. Why would they possibly have a need for those skills?"

"Why did you apply if you were skeptical they could use you?"

"I have eight brothers and sisters, most of them younger than me. That's a lot of mouths to feed even on a farm. Government and war industry jobs pay well. So, I filled out the paper and took the test. This is where they sent me." She rubbed the dirt from a small stone. "I do have a head for figures; you know math problems."

"Ugh. You mean like those awful word problems I struggled through in high school? If two trains left two different stations twelve miles apart, how long until they ran into each other, or some such nonsense? Who needs to know that?"

"Maybe these folks."

The sky darkened, and gray clouds scudded overhead. Emily shivered. "The classes on disguising myself were interesting. And not just wigs and clothing but how to develop habits and mannerisms. I could become a whole different person after the war."

"What would your family think about that?"

"Same as they always do. I made a wrong decision." She huffed out a breath. "Enough about me. What's your favorite class so far?"

"Propaganda. The psychological aspect of trying to influence people. Fascinating. Talk about a skill that comes in handy. I could get my husband to do whatever I wanted him to."

"You're married?" Emily's gaze whipped toward Martha.

"No. I mean when I get one."

"Good luck with that. I'm going it alone. I don't want a husband. Just one more person telling me what to do." She shook her head. "No, after we've won this war, I'm not going home. Maybe I'll stay overseas. I wish they'd tell us where we're going to be stationed."

"They've got to see who's left at the end before they can do that."

Emily glanced at her watch and leapt to her feet. "And if I don't get going, I'm going to be the next victim kicked out."

"What's your class?"

"Tactics and field craft. A fancy name for fighting..." She shuddered. "And killing. Necessary skills if they send me behind the lines, but frightening to think about." Would this be the class that washed her out? She licked her lips, then waved over her shoulder, and trotted toward the two-story brick house, her legs eating up the distance in moments. Racing up the steps, she yanked open the door and hurried down the hallway, coming to a stop a few feet before the classroom.

She patted her hair into place, tucked in her blouse, and ran a hand over her pants. A glance at the clock told her she had thirty seconds to spare. She grinned and entered the room. The only vacant seat was front and center. So much for slipping along the side and into a chair in the back.

"Miss Strealer. Nice of you to join us."

Her jaw dropped, and she stared at the instructor. The Clark Gable lookalike from the airplane leaned against the desk, his face stern.

———————————————

Gerard swallowed a grin. He couldn't let Miss Strealer see how much he enjoyed her discomfort. Since seeing her name on the roster two days ago, he'd had time to adjust to the knowledge of their paths crossing again. Stunned at the thought of the gorgeous young woman parachuting behind enemy lines, he reviewed her file to determine why the agency selected her.

He'd recognized the woman's intelligence on the plane, but her record spoke volumes about her potential. Yes, her language skills and knowledge of the French people were impeccable, but her aptitude scores were higher than every student in her group. Her fine motor skills exceeded his own. She excelled on the intuition tests and passed the psychology evaluation with flying colors.

All well and good, but would she be able to kill a man with her bare hands?

Probably not. Her timidity on the plane during takeoff then during the turbulence incident didn't bode well. It was better for her to fail here and be sent on her way than to put her in a situation from which she couldn't recover.

"Welcome, everyone. Congratulations on making it this far. You are among the brightest America has to offer, and we appreciate your willingness to do your bit for the war effort, as they say. Most of your training has been book learning, but that's about to change. The next five weeks will be the most physically challenging of the course, probably more demanding than you've ever experienced. You will be exhausted at the end of each day. You'll need to push yourself beyond what you ever thought possible." His gaze swept the room, then he zeroed in on Miss Strealer's expression. "This training will make the difference between whether you live or die in the field."

Her eyes widened, and her eyebrows shot up.

He had to give her credit for maintaining her composure. She didn't gasp or go pale like some of the other female students. Did she have the fortitude for this after all?

"Anyone want to back out at this point? No one will blame you if you are unwilling to put your life on the line." He pointed to a pair of women in the back who had exchanged a fearful glance at his comment. "How about you ladies? Want to stay?"

"Yes, sir." They spoke in unison.

They wouldn't last the week. "Fine." He gestured to a smug-looking young man lounging in his chair. "What about you, tough guy? Think you've got what it takes?"

"Absolutely. I'm from the Bowery. Nothing more dangerous than that."

Gerard narrowed his eyes. "We'll see about that." He sauntered forward until he stood inches from Miss Strealer. Crossing his arms, he peered down his nose at her. "And you? Can you handle crawling in the dirt, running for hours wearing a pack, or escaping detection from tracker dogs?"

She sat up, ramrod straight, laid down her pencil, and glared at him. "Yes, sir. Any reason to believe I can't?"

"That remains to be seen."

Her face pinked, but she continued to stare him down. She did seem to have gumption, but would her grit and spunk be enough to keep her alive longer than the six-week average lifespan of a radio operator?

He rubbed his hands together. "All right, enough conversation. Let's get cracking." Gerard clicked on the overhead projector then dimmed the lights. Moving to the screen, he poked a photograph of a small building. "The first topic we're going to discuss is how to attack an enemy-occupied house. Needless to say, surprise is crucial in these situations. Without it, your mission has a greater chance of failure."

Holding up his thumb, he said, "First, there must be a detailed preliminary reconnaissance of the approaches to the house and the house itself." His index finger went up. "Second, there must be a definite plan of action to which *everyone* adheres. No mavericks, no gunslingers." Gerard shot a look at the young man from New York. "Got that, Bowery?"

The recruit nodded.

Gerard clapped his hands, the sound sharp in the silence. "Now, if the group is going to avoid casualties, speed and aggression must be used as soon as the action begins. Lastly, it is essential that every allowance be made by the leader for the original plan to go awry. Be prepared for the worst, because if something can go wrong, there's a strong possibility it will. That's when your real mettle comes into play."

With a flourish, he stabbed the windows and door on the house's image then swapped the Mylar sheet with a photograph of the back of the building. "Lots of ways into this place. Who has an idea about the means of ingress?"

"One of the windows in the back?" A timid suggestion rose from the middle of the group.

"Nope, you're dead. No one can enter quickly, and you're an easy target as soon as you get in. More often than not, you have to jump down when entering through a window."

"The roof. Definitely the roof."

"Excellent, Bowery. It is the most advantageous route because you can drive the enemy lower, and he can't roll any grenades on top of you. However, before you congratulate yourself, be aware it's next to impossible to get there undetected because you are bound to make noise, no matter how hard you try not to. So, you're probably dead, too."

Miss Strealer held up her hand.

"What say you, Miss Strealer?"

She licked her lips.

He blinked so as not to stare at her alluring mouth. Get a grip, Lucas. "Well?"

"Uh, the back door because it's less likely to be defended, at least as strongly as the front?"

"Is that a question or a statement? Seems like a definite maybe."

Her left eyebrow rose, and her chin jutted out. "A statement." She cleared her throat. "Most times the back has better coverage because the landscaping isn't as trimmed or as well cared for."

"Very good. That's correct. If you can't enter via a skylight in the roof, the back door is your second best option." He tossed a glance at her. "Congratulations, Miss Strealer. You're not dead…yet."

He wasn't sure how he felt about that statement.

## Chapter Four

"Again! And get it right this time!"

Emily bit her lip and blinked back tears. She would not let Major Lucas see her distress. He seemed to take perverse pleasure in making things more difficult for her than for the other students. While her classmates were indoors, she'd been outside all day, the last hour in fading daylight working on what he called concealment. Growing up, she'd called it hide-and-seek, and the game was much more fun than the current nightmare in which he was the hunter, and she was the prey.

"Yes, sir." She crept deeper into the copse of trees attempting to walk on soundless feet. The temperatures had dropped well below freezing, and her extremities no longer had any feeling. Her breath and pounding heart were loud in her ears. Could he hear them? Bending, she slithered between the branches of a large, prickly shrub then pressed her back against the massive trunk of an oak tree.

What had the manual said? "Shadows are the most difficult problem in the whole of camouflage, whether a man or airplane factory, but once their importance is realized, half the battle is won." She felt like she'd already been in battle.

Stifling the urge to massage the aches from her back and calves, Emily straightened her spine and peered into the dim woods. She stepped forward, and a branch snapped underfoot, loud as a firecracker. She cringed and waited for the major's shout of derision that she'd failed again.

What sort of assignment would have her traipsing through the woods like a modern-day Daniel Boone? She was a translator not a Sherpa. There couldn't be any possible use for training her to ford rivers, trek through forests, or scale mountains, but all recruits received the same instruction.

"Miss Strealer."

Emily jumped at the voice only a foot away. Major Lucas managed to reach her side without making any noise. She sighed and anticipated his reprimand.

He removed the black wool cap from his head and ran a hand over his closely shorn hair. "Miss Strealer, you're a slender woman. How is it that you make the noise of a man three times your size? Have you studied the chapters I asked you to?"

"Yes."

"Then why can't you conceal yourself correctly? You seem intelligent enough, yet you're the only student who continues to fail at this assignment. What is the problem?"

His eyes, normally shards of blue crystals, were black and unreadable in the darkness that had fallen over them like a cloak.

"I don't know, okay?" She frowned and flapped her arms. "I've practically memorized the book, yet when I try to implement the techniques, I'm all thumbs…or in this case…feet." A giggle escaped, and she clamped her lips together.

"Now is not the time for joking."

"You're right, but I have no answer for you. Granted, I wasn't in the Girl Scouts, so I didn't have a chance to earn a wilderness badge. I bet you were a Boy Scout and even made Eagle Scout. I'm a city girl. I can weave through the thickest crowd of pedestrians without injury or secure a cab with a flick of my wrist. Who knew the forest could make so much noise? It's a mystery. And as to finding my way? There are no landmarks to speak of. It's a wonder I haven't been lost, never to be seen again."

"Are you finished?" Arms crossed, his breath came out in puffs of steam.

His musky scent of Bay Rum assailed her nose, and the planes of his face were silhouetted in the moonlight. How could he be so maddening and so attractive at the same time?

She mimicked his stance. "Apparently."

"Look, I think you can do this, but you have to believe you can as well, otherwise it's never going to work. Ninety percent of learning a skill is in your head. Once you tell yourself you can do it, execution follows."

"You've never struggled with anything, have you?"

"What?"

"Has every task you've ever tried to do come easily? Frankly, I disagree with you about mind over matter. Sometimes a person doesn't have the innate ability."

"But it can be taught." Major Lucas tilted his head.

"Perhaps, but you didn't answer my question."

"What question?"

"Have you always excelled at anything you've tried to do?"

He ducked his head and shrugged.

"I'll take that as a yes." Emily rubbed her forehead. "I want to get this right, but despite your best efforts and mine, I continue to mess up."

"The bottom line is something has to change in order to succeed. I suggest you start with your attitude."

She stiffened. This venture was no different than being at home. Someone judging her abilities and telling her what to do. Treating her like a kid. Maybe she should quit and find somewhere else to serve. Somewhere they would value what she could do.

---

Gerard shoved his hands into his front pockets. He'd made her angry. That was obvious from the way she'd drawn herself up and lifted her chin. He couldn't see her face in the inky darkness, but her posture told him what he needed to know. The girl was smart as a whip. Too bad she couldn't seem to get out of her own way. He'd seen other recruits with the same problem. Dangerous in combat, that trait proved to be fatal in an operative.

"You're upset because you feel like I've insulted you. That's not the case. I'm your instructor. It's my job to qualify you for fieldwork. The kind of work that puts your life and the lives of others on the line. The only way to cheat death is to be fully prepared for any contingency, no matter how remote the possibility is of it occurring. If you're ready when the worst scenario actually occurs, you've got a chance to make it out alive." He nudged her shoulder with his. "Focus that anger, and prove to yourself that you have what it takes. If you think I don't believe in you, prove me wrong."

"Why are you being nice to me? I don't deserve special treatment." Her voice faltered and came out in a whisper.

His heart squeezed. Who had hurt her to the point that she had little trust in others or herself? "Everyone should have a second chance." He almost laughed out loud. His presence here was evidence of that. "I see potential in you, and I'd like to help you reach it. We've done enough physical training for tonight, so head inside and get cleaned up. Then grab your manual, and we'll review it over a cup of coffee. How does that sound?"

She stared at him for a long moment, but he couldn't see her expression. Finally, she nodded, and he released the breath he didn't realize he was holding.

"Excellent." He pulled a small flashlight from his pocket and turned it on with a click. "Follow me."

"Isn't tutoring me cheating, Major?"

He chuckled. "Perhaps, but sometimes that's the best way to win."

––––––––––––––––•–––––––––––––––

"Sorry to keep you waiting, Major."

Gerard turned, and his eyes widened. Freshly scrubbed, Emily's face shone. No makeup colored her complexion, yet her beauty would give any Hollywood starlet a run for her money. Dressed in a skirt and blouse, she wore flats, and her hair was pulled into a ponytail.

He blinked. He was staring like a schoolboy. She must think him a simpleton. "It's no problem." For a second, he held out his arm to escort her, then he motioned toward the hallway on the other side of the foyer. "With any luck, we won't get the dregs in the coffeepot."

"If we do, I'm sure you'll come up with a solution, Major."

"Or perhaps this will be another test of your ingenuity, Miss Strealer."

She giggled, and he smiled. It was good to see her earlier reticence gone.

The dining hall was sparsely populated. Good. They'd have some modicum of privacy. He led her to the coffee station, where several large percolators stood among dozens of heavy white mugs. Government issue.

He quickly filled the cups then led her toward a table next to the windows. "All right, Miss Strealer, here is your next test. Which seat should you take?"

"I don't remember this being in the manual."

Gerard shrugged. "Not everything you need to know is in the textbook. Sometimes experience is the best teacher."

A moment passed, then she dropped into the seat that faced the room. "I picked this one because it's nighttime, and I could be seen from outside. I can also watch the room from this vantage point. Although my preference would be not to sit near the window at all." She looked up, nibbling her lower lip.

"Very good. Your decision should always be based on the circumstances." He raised the cup and took a tentative sip. Hot and bitter, the coffee burned its way down his throat. Wrinkling his nose, he set down the beverage and licked his lips. He'd had worse, but not by much. Even the caffeine content wasn't worth imbibing.

"You shouldn't play poker, Major." Emily drank from her mug. "I was raised not to show an adverse response to bad coffee. See how I smile after I drink as if this were the best brew I've ever had? A genteel women never gives away her thoughts."

"And is that you? A genteel woman?"

She rolled her eyes then lowered her gaze and studied the dark brown brew. "Hardly. However, that's my mother's dream for me. A dream that thus far has gone unrealized when I became a teacher then left home to follow my own path." She took another swallow from her cup. Running her thumb up and down its side, she cocked her head. "Enough about me. What did you leave behind, other than piloting, to do your bit for the war effort?"

"Your parents didn't approve of your vocational choice? Teaching is an honorable profession. You are guiding and molding future generations. What did they prefer for you?"

"A good marriage."

"Oh. And you don't wish to marry?"

"Perhaps someday, but when I do wed, it will be because I am in love with the man, not because the relationship is advantageous."

"Are your folks really that mercenary?" He narrowed his eyes. No wonder this girl didn't trust anyone. Her family was going to auction her off to the highest bidder. He'd have skedaddled, too.

She blew out a loud breath. "Probably not, but they controlled my life with tight fists criticizing many of my decisions and activities. I'm of age. Bad enough I was still living at home, but they seemed to feel that gave them license to dictate my comings and goings. I was stagnating."

"So, you're here to prove you're grown up?"

"What? No." Her eyes glinted. "I needed to do more with my life, something that made a difference. Something other than helping high school students earn their fine arts credit. Most of them will forget the language within months of graduating." Her lips twisted. "Hardly an auspicious career...teaching a skill soon forgotten."

"But there are other life lessons you pass along in the classroom, right?"

"Yes. What's your point? Why are you trying to convince me that I was in a glorious and noble career? Are you trying to change my mind about finishing the course? I thought you were here to ensure I passed." Her words were like steel.

He'd offended her again. With a shake of his head, he pushed away his coffee mug, then crossed his arms. "I just want to make sure you understand the ramifications of your decision of finishing the course. I'm a military man. My job is to put my life on the line every moment of every day. You're a civilian. Intelligent, yes, but are you smart enough to stay alive?"

Emily shoved back her chair and stood. "Make up your mind, Major Lucas. Believe in me or not, but stop waffling. One minute you say I can do this and offer to assist me, the next you're casting aspersions on my abilities."

"I'm—"

"Let me finish before you start making excuses about your behavior. I can do this. Yes, I've struggled a bit. But I will succeed, even without your help. You know nothing about me. Sure, you may have read my file, but there is more to me than words on a page." She picked up the manual and coffee cup. "Now, if you'll excuse me, Major, I have to study."

She swept past him like royalty, back straight and head held high. The fresh scent of her soap lingered in the air.

Closing his eyes, he raked his hands through his hair. She was a spitfire, but her sensitivity to criticism and obeying orders could be a problem. If she didn't learn to respect the chain of command, she wouldn't last long in the field.

## Chapter Five

Gerard stuffed his hands into his front pockets and skirted the grassy meadow where dozens of recruits were practicing modes of stealth. He surveyed the men and women in various stages of creeping, climbing, and hiding around the facsimiles of houses, cars, trees, and bushes, his gaze searching for Miss Strealer's petite figure.

Where was she? Had she decided to pack it in despite last night's pronouncement?

Movement in the distant trees caught his attention, perhaps one of the many white-tailed deer that called the surrounding forest home. Shrubs shifted, then nothing. No, not wildlife. The motion was too studied. One of the instructors? Maybe, but the other two men in charge of field craft were also U.S. Army. Certainly their concealment skills would be better than whomever was skulking amid the foliage.

He crossed his arms and waited. Squinting, he peered into the trees. Minutes passed. Maybe it was one of the smaller woodland creatures. With a shrug, he turned toward the brick plantation home that housed the commander's office.

Then he saw her.

Dressed in black pants and a dark green, long-sleeved shirt, Miss Strealer emerged at the edge of the timberline. Her hair was stuffed into a wool cap, and her face was smudged with dirt. She smiled, and although more than fifty yards away, he could read her look of triumph. A moment later, Major Warren Hellman appeared behind her.

His jaw clenched. Since when did Hellman provide one-on-one instruction?

Forty-five if he was a day, the major exuded an annoying mixture of charm and arrogance. A career man, he'd transferred to the OSS from a military intelligence unit and acted as if he were the lone savior to the fledgling organization. Granted, its reputation was not secure yet, and many of the higher-ups didn't seem to trust what some referred to as the department of dirty tricks, but the agency would succeed because of Director William Donovan's leadership, not some debonair military man playing at being a spy.

Hellman clapped Miss Strealer on the back, his hand lingering just short of inappropriate.

A growl rumbled in Gerard's throat, and he started toward the pair, then froze. She'd light him up worse than the previous evening if he intervened.

Miss Strealer pulled off the hat, and her hair tumbled onto her shoulders. She tucked the cinnamon-colored tresses behind her ears. They tramped toward one of the water stations. The major said something, and she laughed.

If he stood gaping at the pair any longer, he'd be caught staring, and that would not do. Gerard whirled toward the worn but beautiful Georgian-style house, its white Doric columns supporting the second-story portico. The white trim and dentil molding needed to be painted, and the dormers along the roofline had seen better days, but the building still managed to maintain a regal bearing.

Stifling the urge to look over his shoulder to see if he'd been spotted, Gerard trotted up the stone steps and marched across the wooden porch. He flung open the door and hurried inside.

A young blonde dressed in a Women's Army Auxiliary Corps uniform sat behind a gleaming desk in the middle of the tiled foyer. Gilt-framed portraits of the owner's ancestors observed the comings and goings with looks of disdain. She held up a finger, warding off his approach, then continued her telephone conversation in muted tones.

He clasped his hands behind his back and rocked on his heels. Would she ever hang up the phone?

A few moments later, she replaced the receiver and looked up. "How may I help you, Major Lucas?"

"I need to see Colonel Frederickson about a matter of great importance. Is he available?"

"Let me check." She pressed the button on the intercom to her right. "Minnie, Major Lucas is here to see the colonel. Does he have room on his schedule for a meeting?"

"What is this regarding?" The tinny voice coming from the small box crackled.

Gerard stepped forward. "One of the recruits, Miss Strealer."

"Just a second."

Minutes passed. The blonde rolled a piece of paper into her typewriter and began pounding on the keys, the staccato noise bouncing off the plaster walls. Gerard stifled the urge to rush up the stairs and barge into the colonel's office. That kind of rogue behavior got him sent here in the first place, but it was a surefire way to get him tossed out.

"Send him up." The disembodied voice broke the silence.

The receptionist's fingers continuing to dance across the keyboard, and she jerked her head toward the stairway.

"Thank you, miss." Gerard hurried upstairs, the rubber soles of his boots squeaking against the marble tread. On the landing, he turned right and made his way to the suite that quartered his commanding officer. He ran a hand over his hair and straightened his spine then went inside the ornate outer room. Another WAAC rose when he appeared and gestured toward Colonel Frederickson's door. The agency might be new, but as a government organization they were just as hierarchy-driven as the army.

He knocked on the doorframe then entered.

Formerly a Pinkerton detective, Theodore Frederickson had been recruited by Director Donovan himself and given the rank of full colonel so no one could question his authority. Somewhere on one side or the other of sixty years old, the man was several inches under six feet but wiry. Gerard had no doubt that whatever his size, he could best anyone.

"Major Lucas, good to see you. Your timing is quite fortuitous. I was just getting ready to send for you." Colonel Frederickson sat on a blue floral Louis XIV couch near a large stone fireplace in which a fire burned brightly, creating a pocket of warmth in the chilly room. "Please sit."

Gerard eyed a pair of dainty chairs with spindly legs. He lowered himself into the closest one, waiting for it to give beneath his weight. When the seat didn't shatter, he leaned back and folded his hands. "You wanted to see me, sir?"

"Yes, I wondered how our latest group of recruits is getting on. I read the reports, but I find a conversation is often more revealing than dry paperwork. Wouldn't you agree?"

"Uh, yes, sir."

"The war is going to heat up, and it is imperative these trainees come up to speed quickly. We also need to know who should be let go. Not everyone is cut out for this organization, and I prefer that we cut them loose sooner rather than later."

"Absolutely, sir. That's actually why I came to see you. It's my belief that Miss Strealer, although brilliant in book learning may not be a good field agent. She's having trouble getting a handle on some of the finer techniques, and she becomes defensive when corrected. Perhaps retaining her as an analyst is the best placement." There. He'd said it, and the decision was out of his hands. Why didn't he feel the satisfaction he'd anticipated?

"Sounds as if she's a bit like you, eh?"

"Sir?"

"I spoke with your former commanding officer, Major Albert. Bruce and I go way back. Attended the same high school then graduated from Harvard together. He's my son's godfather."

Gerard swallowed. What had the major said about him? "Then you must be close."

"Like brothers. Nothing we wouldn't do for each other. That's why you're here. He told me about a rather unruly pilot he had. Someone who had trouble toeing the line. A bright chap but somewhat of a bounder. Thought he knew more than his superiors and often argued with them. The final straw was an incident with a Major Quigley." Major Frederickson's piercing glare seemed to nail Gerard to the chair. "Sound familiar?"

Face heating, Gerard licked his lips. "Yes, sir."

"I know Quigley is a pretentious clod, but he is a superior officer. It is imperative that chain of command be adhered to, no matter how much of an idiot is giving the order. Instead of undermining the man in front of others, you should have held your tongue and spoken with someone in authority. At a minimum, you should have been demoted for the incident. He wanted you to be court-martialed, you know, but Bruce sees a quality in you worth saving."

"I appreciate the opportunity, sir."

"Bruce is a good judge of character. He indicated putting you in the stockade for the duration would have been a waste of skills and intelligence. I'm inclined to agree, but you're a bit of a maverick, Major Lucas. That trait only goes so far in this organization. Yes, we're highly irregular, but even the OSS has protocols that must be followed."

"I understand." Gerard kneaded his fingers. Why had the conversation become about him, rather than the recruits?

"Now, before we discuss the wayward Miss Strealer, tell me about her classmates. Most seem to be getting high marks and are fitting in, but there are a couple who may need to be processed out."

Gerard nodded. "Roper and Crowder should be let go. They are a danger to themselves and others. I can give you specifics, if you like."

Major Hellman waved his hand in a dismissive gesture. "No, I've seen their test scores, and if it's the pair I watched in the quadrangle yesterday during target practice, then I agree with your assessment. One had flaming red hair, the other dark headed. Didn't seem to take things seriously."

"That's them, sir." Gerard cocked his head. "What if they talk about us after they're gone?"

"Won't happen. They're not being discharged for exactly that reason. We'll continue to control them. I hope they like cold weather. Our misfits get transferred to one of the bases in Alaska."

Gerard winced. Not somewhere he'd want to spend any amount of time.

"What about the remaining newcomers?"

"O'Reilly and Sambra seem exceptionally well suited to the organization. They aced every one of their tests, and their ingenuity at handling the fieldwork surpasses anything I've ever seen. I believe they could handle just about any situation in which they find themselves."

"Excellent. That's my assessment as well. What about Brannon? His test scores are not top of the heap, but he seems to be succeeding with his field tactics."

"I'm not sure what the issue is with him, sir. When I quiz him verbally, he answers every question correctly, but having to write things down seems to be difficult. Perhaps he just learns differently, sir. I think he'd be an asset as an operative and worth cultivating."

"Agreed." Major Hellman narrowed his eyes. "Tell me about Miss Strealer. What should we do with her? I'd hate to send her to the tundra."

"Permission to speak freely, sir?"

"Granted."

Gerard shifted in the seat and wiped his damp palms on his pants. "She's too pretty to be used as an agent. She'd be too noticeable. Agents should blend in, especially the women. Every Frenchman and German would follow her like a lapdog. With her grasp of the French language and culture, we'll be best served if she remains here as an analyst."

"You think she's attractive, do you?"

"Yes, beautiful, in fact." Gerard nodded as he pictured her heart-shaped face.

"Perfect." A grin split Major Hellman's face, and he rubbed his hands together. "The Germans will never believe we'd send someone with her looks. She won't blend in, so they'll think she's a native."

"You're sending her to Germany?" Gerard's heart skittered. "I didn't realize we had agents there."

"Not Germany. Occupied France. She'll be a radio operator."

"That's the most dangerous position in the organization. I'm not sure she's ready."

"You have plenty of time to get her ready. She's leaves in ten days, and you're going with her. We haven't finished creating your cover story, but suffice it to say you'll pretend to be married."

## Chapter Six

"What do you mean we're going to pretend to be married?" Emily gaped at Major Lucas, her heart pounding. Her first mission, and not only was she going to be saddled with her devastatingly handsome yet arrogant instructor, but she was supposed to impersonate being his wife. What was the colonel thinking when he'd made that decision?

"Just like it sounds. We're to be parachuted into France and make our way to Paris, where you'll operate the radio, and I'll work with Resistance members. There's no concerted effort on their part, so the underground forces are not as effective as they could be. The French are progressive but not enough to accept a man and woman living together without the benefit of marriage. Assumptions will be made that you're a prostitute. Does that suit your sensibilities better?"

She reared back. "Of course not. But why do we have to go together. Paris is a large city. You could stay and work in one location, and I could set up in another."

"Stop questioning the order. Colonel Hellman has his reasons for the assignment. We have to trust his judgment."

"Look me in the eye, and tell me you weren't shocked and a bit put off." Emily crossed her arms and glared at him. "That you went along with the idea and didn't challenge him."

Gerard's gaze slid to the floor.

"Yeah, that's what I thought, so don't act all high and mighty while I try to digest the fact that I've actually made the grade and will be sent behind enemy lines with a man I barely know under the auspices of being his wife." Perspiration broke out along her hairline. Her stomached clenched, and she licked her dry lips. Her dream of being an agent and making a difference was coming true. Would she succeed or become a casualty? Would she beat the odds and outlive the six-week lifespan of an operator?

She pivoted on her heel and walked to the window. Outside, the latest group of recruits was practicing maneuvers, one of which was the silent kill. *Lord, help me.*

Major Lucas approached from behind. "Look, I know you're surprised, but do you have to act like working with me is the worst thing that could have happened to you?"

"I'm sorry." Emily blew out a breath and turned to face him. "That was rude of me. It's not you. It's me. As usual, I'm hearing all the naysayers in my head trying to convince me that I'm not fit for this mission and that my decision is foolhardy." She rubbed at her arms, suddenly chilled. "You couldn't possibly understand. Confidence has never been an issue for you, has it? You must think I'm a sniveling girl who should be home rolling bandages."

"First of all, I've had moments of doubt during my career, many of which occurred during this assignment. Secondly, you're wrong about my assessment of you. I believe you're an intelligent, brave woman who is willing to risk her life for her country." His crystal-blue eyes glinted in the sunshine pouring through the glass panes and seemed to caress her face. "I admire you for volunteering. And you can do this. The colonel would not have selected you otherwise."

In thirteen weeks of training, his baritone voice had never held softness before. What would it be like to have him truly care? Her face warmed, and she blinked to dismiss the thought. "Thanks for those encouraging words. It means a lot. You were one of my toughest instructors." She chuckled. "I hated you for that, but now that I'm going to face the enemy, I know I'm fully prepared. If I fail, it won't be your fault."

He grinned. "If you hadn't disliked me, I wouldn't have been doing my job."

His smile lit up his face and washed away the lines of stress that never seemed to disappear from his expression. Her breath caught. Did he realize how good looking he was? A fake relationship with a Clark Gable lookalike. What was she getting herself into? She'd have to pretend to love him while guarding her heart against the real thing.

Lord, are Cora and Doris right? Is working for the OSS an attempt to prove myself rather than follow Your plan for me? I don't think it is.

The world is fighting malevolent forces, and I want to do my part to defeat this terrible evil. Perhaps I didn't consider everything when I applied. Now, I'll have to lie and practice deceit in my role as the major's wife. Are You okay with that, Father?

Nothing.

She nibbled her lower lip. No peace flooded her in a confirmation that God was in sync with her assignment. What had she expected? A cloud and a voice or a visit from an angel?

"You okay?" Major Lucas touched her shoulder.

"Yes, still processing the information, but I'll be fine. I have to be." She straightened her spine. "When do we depart?"

"Ten days. If you want, Colonel Hellman will give you a seven-day pass so you can go home before we leave."

"Spending a week with my family is the last thing I want to do, Major. Their negativity would undo most of our hard work." She shook her head. "No trip home for me, but I wouldn't mind heading back to Washington to sightsee."

"I'll make the arrangements." He cleared his throat. "I'm not the perfect soldier you seem to think I am. This transfer is my last chance at not being demoted or drummed out of the army. I told off one too many superior officers. Fortunately, my last commanding officer wasn't a career man and saw my behaviors as an asset to the OSS, so he managed to get me reassigned. I didn't realize how much I disliked the armed forces until I got here." He rubbed his forehead. "And now I can do serious damage to the Nazis, more than just shooting up a few of them. We can thwart their plans and disrupt whole campaigns. Perhaps shorten this blasted war by a few months. Then my brother's death at the hands of the Germans might mean something."

"I'm sorry about your brother. Losing him must have been difficult." Tears rushed forward. Now she understood the constant pain that lurked in his eyes. Pain she wanted to help him erase.

———————————

Gerard shook his head. Why had he bared his soul like that? Now she had information she could hold against him or talk about in the event she was captured. Her face held compassion, but once they spent enough time together, she'd realize what a loser he was. That his brother's death was his fault.

"Yeah, but lots of guys have lost loved ones." He hardened his voice. "I've got to focus on the job and not let personal feelings get in the way."

She squeezed his arm then tucked her hands into the pockets of her slacks. His skin tingled at the warmth of her fingers that permeated his cotton shirt. "And sometimes you've got to let your feelings drive you to the goal."

"You're right. I guess we both have motives for this assignment." He gestured toward the coffee station at the end of the room. "Can I get you a cup? We should review our cover story before you leave for Washington." He pulled a folded sheet of paper from his breast pocket.

"They've given us the basics, but the more of our genuine background we incorporate, the better. We'll have to remember fewer lies that way."

"Coffee is great, but is the kitchen still open? I'm famished. We'll be living on starvation rations in a couple of weeks. I've got to eat while I can."

"I could use some food, too. After you."

She sauntered across the room, oblivious to the stares from some of the male agents. Hard to believe she was unaware of her beauty. Would he be able to keep his emotional distance after they arrived in the field? Pretending to be in love with her might be the most dangerous part of the mission.

They grabbed sandwiches and soup and made their way to a secluded table in the corner.

Gerard picked up his spoon and sipped the flavorful vegetable beef soup. What would civilians think if they knew how well the agents were fed. He glanced at Miss Strealer, and his hand froze. Her head was bowed, and her lips moved silently. His face warmed. She'd think him an oaf for not asking a blessing.

She looked up with a smile then leaned over her food and took a deep breath. "I was only partially joking when I mentioned how we'd eat in France, but now I realize how true it is. I imagine we won't have access to anything like this." She gestured to his hand still midair between the bowl and his mouth. "Better get seconds if you can."

He hadn't prayed since Major Hellman notified him about his brother's death. Anyone who believed God was on the Allies' side wasn't paying attention. He allowed decent men to perish every day. No, God definitely didn't care. If the good guys were going to win, they'd have to count on clever strategy and tactics.

"Do you not like your food, Major?" Miss Strealer's soft voice broke through his ruminations.

"Sorry. Just caught up in thought." Gerard dipped the utensil back in the bowl and gave himself a mental slap. Focus Lucas. The mission is everything. He forced a smile. "So, tell me about yourself. I know you have three sisters, but how did you decide to become a French teacher? I daresay most little girls don't grow up with a wish to teach a foreign language."

She giggled then dabbed her mouth with the napkin before laying it on the table. "Our next door neighbors were from France. I'm not sure why they relocated to the United States, but they had lived there for years. We played with their kids, and the whole lot of them spoke French at home, so my sisters and I were exposed to it. We learned about their homeland and picked up the language." She shrugged. "Fortunately, my parents believed in educating their daughters, so when they asked what I wanted to study at college, I chose French and decided to be a teacher so I could share what I'd learned. Who knew I would end up here? What about you? You must speak the language or they wouldn't send you."

"I do, but my reasoning is not as noble as yours. I needed an elective in high school, and I had a crush on a certain young lady. I managed to find out her schedule and registered for the same class. Turns out I have an ear for languages. I picked up French quickly and easily, but the girl never panned out." He rolled his eyes. "And now here I am with another girl from high school French."

"Touché." She held up her cup in a mock toast and laughed, her face turning a lovely shade of pink.

Gerard clinked his coffee mug with hers. If he wasn't careful, it might be high school all over again.

## Chapter Seven

Emily tightened her grip on the handle of her satchel and grabbed the handrail of the metal staircase leading into the airplane. Her stomach clenched. Would turbulence rock this craft like it had during her first flight? How did air cause such a large steel craft to buck and bump like a slip of paper on a windy day? She took a deep breath and climbed the steps, a shiver slithering up her spine. The dawn's murky sunlight did nothing to warm her.

She sat down and shoved her bag underneath her seat. A commercial airliner before the war, the plane had been converted for troop transport. Smoothing her skirt, she looked up as Gerard sat next to her. Over the four days of working on their cover story, he was no longer Major Lucas in her mind. His name finally rolled off her tongue with ease, and she liked how it felt.

He winked as he settled in beside her and crossed his legs.

Her breath caught, and she peeked out the window. Shadowy figures rushed across the tarmac toward the aircraft while others performed myriad tasks. Small trucks darted between airplanes and the terminal. The sun continued to rise, breaking through the morning fog.

Trees materialized at the edge of the taxiway. Would she live to see her beloved country again? If so, how long before she returned home?

"A franc for your thoughts." Gerard's voice sounded close to her ear.

With a start, she turned. His eyes had darkened to cobalt with concern. She forced a smile and sat back in her seat. "Just wondering what the future holds. Having been with the military, you're a seasoned traveler. As of three months ago, I'd never left my state, and now I'm getting ready to fly to Europe…perhaps never to come back." She shrugged. "The feeling is rather daunting."

"I understand. I felt the same way the first time I shipped out." He squeezed her arm. "Too bad we won't be spending any time in England. I think you'd love it. London is a fantastic city with thousand-year-old history everywhere you look. The villages are beautiful and quaint, many of which have castles nearby. Maybe after the war, you can visit."

"I'd like that. I also want to explore France. The photographs in my textbooks show a gorgeous country. But now, the citizens are suffering under the heavy boots of the Germans. The few news reports I've seen indicate the people are starving because the Nazis are availing themselves of most of the supplies. So sad."

"Agreed, which is why our mission is vital, and you're ready. You do know that, right? You've studied hard and are fully prepared. I have no reservations about your skills and knowledge."

Emily ducked her head. "Thanks for saying that. We got off to a rocky start, but I couldn't have completed the courses without you." She sighed. "I wish I had a report card to send home, so I could prove I'm not a total failure."

"You've nothing to prove. It's your family's fault they don't believe in you."

"Ladies and gentlemen, fasten your seat belts. We've been approved for takeoff."

Her eyes widened, and she nibbled her lower lip, then pressed them together. It was a habit she needed to quit.

The aircraft rumbled along the taxiway then turned onto the runway. Awkward and cumbersome on the ground, the plane gathered speed and lifted, engines screaming.

Emily pressed a hand against her middle in anticipation of the butterflies that would also take flight, but her nerves remained steady. She grinned at Gerard. "After all you've put me through, I guess flying is easy."

He chuckled and pulled out a deck of cards. "How about a few games of gin rummy to pass the time. We've got a long journey ahead of us."

"Prepare to lose, Major, um, I mean, Gerard. This is one area in which I'm highly skilled."

"Would you like to make a wager, Emily?"

"And take your hard-earned money? It wouldn't be fair."

"Overconfidence is dangerous. And never underestimate your opponent."

Emily giggled and held out her hand. "You're on."

He enveloped her hand in his calloused palm and shook it.

Tingles shot up her arm, and she shivered. She glanced at his face, and the muscle in his jaw flexed. Had he felt the sensation too? Extricating her hand, she swallowed and pointed to the deck. Business. She had to remember their partnership was strictly business. "Deal 'em, Major."

———————————◆———————————

Gerard shuffled the cards, the softness of her hands still lingering on his palms. He studied her through his peripheral vision, her face a mixture of excitement and trepidation. Despite his efforts to ignore the adrenaline coursing through his veins, he probably looked the same way. All the men did before a campaign. A medic once told him the chemical was great in small doses, responsible for sharpening his senses, but too much would render him helpless.

The aircraft reached cruising altitude, and the shriek of the engines reduced to a dull roar. He put his briefcase on his lap and dealt them each a hand before laying down the remainder of the deck. "You first."

Emily picked up a card, tucked it in her hand, and then discarded a two of diamonds.

Gerard tapped his index finger on his chin while he considered his strategy.

She poked at the pile. "I'd say we haven't got all day, but I guess we do."

"And possibly all night. I forgot to ask the pilot how long this trip would take." He selected a card, glanced at it, then put it on the discard pile.

"I'm trying not think about the fact we're flying over water for the majority of the flight."

"More phobias?"

Her face pinked, and she took her turn. "No, somehow it just seems worse to crash in the water than on land. At least on terra firma we'd have somewhere to travel to if we survived. On the water we'd be floating on endless ocean."

He cocked his head. "Do you always consider the worst-case scenario?"

With a shrug, Emily laid down her cards. "Gin."

"What? How can you have won already?"

She laughed. "It's your fault. You dealt me a hand that was almost complete."

"See if you can do a better job."

"Don't mind if I do." She scooped up the deck and shuffled, her eyes sparkling, and her face flushed. She distributed the cards, laying each one down with a snap.

"You are much more competitive than I realized."

"Who said never underestimate your opponent?" She giggled, bell-like, then rubbed her chin. "Oh, wait. That was you."

"Touché." He cocked his head. "Seems to me we've been here before. The Germans don't know what they've got coming."

"Hey, Major." Jensen leaned across the aisle and slapped Gerard's knee. "You two going to yammer the whole time? Some of us are trying to get some shut-eye."

"Mind your Ps and Qs, Jensen."

"Hard to, with all the noise you're making."

"You're jealous because you're stuck with Tully, whose claim to fame is how many hot dogs he can eat at one sitting, while I'm teamed with the lovely Emily. Guess you should have paid closer attention in class."

The stocky man snorted a laugh and touched two fingers to his forehead in mock salute. "Tully and I are going to have more fun than you two, stuck with the Frogs. I'd rather work with the Brits. Bet the food is better."

"But not the wine."

"I'm a beer man, myself."

"Why am I not surprised?"

"Hey—"

"All right, gentlemen, please remember we're on the same side." Emily waved her hands in the air.

"Beg your pardon, miss."

Jensen cleared his throat. "Rumor has it that you two are pretending to be married. I haven't seen any lovey-dovey behavior. You might want to practice before you get there. You know, cuddle up together, kiss." He closed his eyes and pursed his lips.

Tully sat up and applauded. "Great idea, Jensen. They should get the hang of kissing each other. Their romance needs to be gen-u-ine. What better time to rehearse than in the privacy of the plane? Come on, Major, lay one on her."

Gerard frowned. The conversation was getting out of control. He glanced at Emily. Her eyes were wide and uncertain, her hands clenched around the deck of cards. He slapped Tully's shoulder. "We don't need any guidance from you, and as far as privacy goes, I don't see any."

"We promise to close our eyes, don't we, Tully?"

"Sure, Major. We won't look."

"Enough, Jensen."

"Kiss her. Kiss her. Kiss her." Jensen clapped his hands in rhythm with his words.

Tully joined him, a sloppy grin on his face. Within seconds, the rest of the passengers were involved.

Gerard's chest tightened. Would a quick peck on her lips put the mayhem to rest? Probably not, but it was worth a try.

He swiveled his neck and met Emily's eyes. Her face had paled, but she held herself erect as if with pride. He grasped her cold, tense hand and pressed it with what he hoped was a reassuring squeeze. Her fingers loosened in his, and her shoulder lifted a fraction. It seemed she was willing to follow his lead and attempt to put the cajoling to rest.

Leaning forward, he touched his lips to hers, their warmth and softness drawing him in. Her pupils dilated, nearly eliminating the emerald green of her irises. He pulled away, and she dropped her gaze. The taste of her remained as he pivoted to the passengers. "Satisfied, Jensen? Let's hope your manners improve by the time we land in London."

Booing filled the plane. Jensen pinched his nose and held his thumb upside down. "You call that a kiss? My little brother could do a better job, and he hasn't graduated high school." He puffed out his chest. "Or you can let me show her how it's done."

"Not a chance." Gerard gritted his teeth.

Emily tapped his arm, and he glanced at her. She tugged his hand, a tiny smile lifting the corner of her mouth. Was she telling him to try again? A chill swept over him. An imperceptible nod moved her head, and her gaze bore into his face.

"We do not have to do this, Emily." His voice was barely above a whisper as he spoke into her ear. "I will not be bullied into acting inappropriately. My upbringing may not have been perfect, but I will treat you with respect and do my best not to hurt you."

"I trust you." Her voice was steady.

"If you're sure—"

"Absolutely. This is ridiculous, and we have nothing to prove, but I will not give them the satisfaction of seeing me back down. Now, kiss me as a proper newlywed husband."

Gerard lowered his head then hesitated a breath away from her mouth. His gaze bore into hers until her lids fluttered shut. His mouth touched hers, and he was again struck by their softness. Her arm slid around his neck, her fingers tangling in his hair. His heart skittered, and he deepened the kiss. Time seemed to freeze and envelope them.

After a long moment, he pulled away, looking into her eyes once again. She stared back, expression clear and without guile. She patted his hand then leaned around him and pointed at Jensen, her face dark. "If you ever treat me like that again, I will personally take you aside and thrash you. Understood?"

Jensen's eyes widened, and he nodded. He whirled in his seat and pulled his cap down over his eyes.

Gerard grinned. This gal was nothing like he'd ever met. Despite the danger, he was suddenly looking forward to the mission as more than a task to complete.

## Chapter Eight

Moonlight enveloped Gerard, and air whistled past his ears as he drifted toward the earth, his parachute ghostly against the night sky. They'd had two days in England to prepare for their drop into France. London was fatigued and dust filled from the Blitz and twelve months of air raids, but the British citizens carried on, proving their resilience to Hitler and his forces.

Gerard searched among the stars for the white expanse of Emily's chute. Fluttering movement to his left, and he twisted his neck to look. Slightly above him and several hundred yards away, she hung among the risers of her rig. *Please give her a soft landing, God.* Gripping his own risers, he lowered his chin then tucked in his elbows. Would the Creator of the universe listen to him? He hadn't prayed in months, and now he was coming forward with a request.

The ground rushed toward him, and he bent his knees in preparation for touchdown. His feet hit soil. Allowing his body to buckle, he rolled to the side to distribute the shock of impact. His breath expelled with a grunt as he came to a stop. A quick inventory—no broken bones.

With practiced motions, he leapt to his feet, then turned to face the canopy. Releasing one of the toggles, he pulled in the other. He ran downwind of the chute, and it collapsed. He stowed the brakes then grabbed the silk and shook it to release any trapped air. He bent, looped the lines, and gathered the chute into his arms. Less than a minute had ticked by.

He looked up.

Emily wafted to the ground and rolled. She jumped up and began to collect her parachute.

A quick glance at the compass strapped to his wrist, then he trotted in her direction. By the time he arrived at her side, she was cradling the silk. He smiled. "You did well. How are you feeling?"

She rubbed her arm. "Like I just dropped out of a plane." She grinned, her teeth flashing in the moon's luminescence.

"Funny, but I guess that means you're okay." Gerard jerked his head toward the edge of the field. "Let's bury these under that thicket then make our way to the rendezvous point." He spoke in a whisper.

She pressed her lips together and nodded.

They hurried toward the bushes, and he pulled aside the branches so she could shove her chute underneath. He made quick work of stowing his own then moved the brush back into place. Satisfied the white fabric was hidden from view, he climbed to his feet and checked the compass again.

Emily unfolded the silk map she carried and tilted it toward the moonlight. Having already committed the geography to memory, he nonetheless studied it. He gave her a curt nod, and she slid the fabric back into the hidden pocket of her jacket.

Gerard located the dirt road indicated on the map, and they set off in a northerly direction. Keeping to the edge so they could duck into the woods at the sound of oncoming traffic, Gerard walked at a fast clip. Curfew was strictly monitored, and if they were caught, it would likely not go well. By all accounts, the Germans rarely believed anyone innocent who was found outside at night, especially during the wee hours.

An hour passed before they arrived at a dilapidated house where they were to meet their contact. The grounds were overgrown, and the building, with its snaggletoothed windows, looked as if a stiff wind could crumple it. Was their go-between inside?

He cleared his throat then produced the screech of a barn owl.

Emily flinched.

Seconds later, an answering shriek returned from behind a copse of trees located about thirty yards from the house. He repeated the call, and a duplicate response sounded.

Excellent. Help was here.

Two shadowy figures emerged from the foliage, each wheeling a pair of bicycles.

Gerard exhaled. Even better. These men were prepared.

The pair handed Gerard and Emily each a bike.

"*Bonsoir.*" Emily smiled as she grasped the handlebars.

The taller of the men dipped his head. "*Bienvenue en France.* We must make haste. The sun won't be up for several hours, but the sooner we reach our destination, the better."

"Oui, monsieur." Gerard swung his leg over the bar and glanced at Emily who'd done the same. Face resolute, she gripped the handlebars, her knuckles white. He nodded to himself. She was a tough one. So far, so good.

They followed the Frenchmen. Miles passed, and perspiration drenched Gerard's shirt and trickled down the sides of his face. The shadowed hulks of houses and barns dotted the landscape.

When they approached a small village, its homes hunched together behind wooden fences, the man who seemed to be in charge parked his bike in front of a small bungalow while his companion waited.

Braking, Gerard squinted through the darkness, the hair on the back of his neck prickling. Were they being watched? Was this a trap?

The guide opened the gate and motioned for Gerard and Emily to dismount. "*Ça y est.* This is where you will be stationed."

"Won't the villagers be surprised or suspicious to see newcomers?" Gerard couldn't shake the feeling that something was amiss. "Especially ones who arrived in the dead of night?"

"*Non.* Those who live in this village do not want the Germans here, in our country. Resistance efforts are not coordinated yet, and even after two years, we are disjointed, but these people have pulled together to do what they can. You will find them cautious, but welcoming. They won't question your identity. I told them you are my sister and brother-in-law."

His guide motioned toward the backyard. "Enough talking. We've been outside too long already." They wheeled their bicycles behind the house and leaned them against the wall beside the door. The guide unlocked the door and pushed it open. Pressing the key into Gerard's hand, he stepped away. "Wait for others to turn on their lights before you do so. Food and supplies are in the kitchen. If you need to contact me, go to the fountain in the middle of the village, and put a slip of paper behind the loose brick in the northern side of the base." He dipped his head. "May God hold you in His hand."

After the man and his partner left, Gerard motioned for Emily to step inside.

Heart pounding, he tilted his head, ears straining for the slightest noise. Why hadn't the Frenchman checked the house before admitting them? Was the village truly a refuge from the Germans who overran the country? He grasped Emily's arm. "Stay here," he whispered. "I want to ensure the house is empty."

She gasped. "Do you think—"

"I don't know, but it would not do for us to be caught unawares. The Frenchman is too trusting for my taste." He patted her shoulder. "I won't be long."

He pulled his gun from the holster around his ankle, unlocked the safety, the click loud in the silence. Eyes burning from trying to see through the darkness, he crept forward on the balls of his feet. He entered each room, opening doors and checking behind curtains. No one. They were alone.

His senses continued to tingle, and he rubbed the back of his neck. With any luck, they were safe, and he was overreacting due to fatigue. He returned to the foyer. "All clear."

Emily let out a loud sigh.

Gerard nodded. "I agree." No need to tell her his concerns. "You can have the bedroom. Get some shut-eye. I'll take watch until first light, then we can swap."

She wrapped her arms around her middle. "As exhausted as I am, I don't think I can sleep. Do you mind if I stay out here?"

"No, the company will be nice."

Turning, she bumped into a chair and stumbled. Arms flailing, she fell against him. He steadied her with his hands, and the floral scent of her shampoo tickled his nose. How could she smell so good after a lengthy plane ride then bicycling through the countryside for miles?

"I'm sorry. I must be more tired than I realized."

He slipped an arm around her shoulder and led her to the couch, dimly visible in the growing light. "Understandable. Lie on the sofa, and I'll take the chair near the window. We can sort things out after sunrise, which looks imminent." Outside the window, streaks of pink and purple decorated the sky. "Looks like our first day on French soil is going to be a beautiful one."

"Hopefully that bodes well for our…uh…visit." Her stomach rumbled, and she giggled. "It won't be too soon for breakfast. Wonder what they left us to eat."

"Nothing extravagant, I assure you."

"I'll take simple. Anything that fills me will be appreciated."

Minutes ticked past, and Gerard stretched, the bones in his spine popping with his movement. He drummed his fingers on his thighs then crossed his arms. Waiting was never his strong suit. Crossing his legs, he jiggled his foot.

"And I thought I was impatient." Emily chuckled.

"Yeah, waiting is the worst part of any mission. Not my best skill." A window across the street illuminated. "Finally." He stood and clicked on the lamp that stood on the end table. "Stay put, and I'll rustle up some grub."

"Now you're John Wayne?"

"Yeah, just call me the Duke." He pretended to doff a large hat in her direction, a wide grin on his face. With a final laugh, he strode into the kitchen and took inventory. Two loaves of bread and a lump of cheese. A half-dozen eggs. Carrots, turnips, artichokes, and potatoes. He'd heard the French were subsisting on vegetables. As sparse as food was in the country, supplies couldn't be adequate in the large cities, especially in occupied Paris where the Germans exhausted the local food resources.

Gerard lit the stove, pulled a frying pan from the hook above the counter, and set it on the burner. Rummaging until he found a bowl and utensils, he cracked the eggs then whipped them with a fork before pouring them into the skillet. He sprinkled bits of cheese on top and scraped the mixture from the bottom as it firmed.

Emily entered the kitchen and dropped into one of the rickety, ladder-back chairs. "That smells divine. Should I continue to keep watch out front?"

"No, I believe we're safe for the time being. Let's eat."

He found a couple of plates and divided the eggs between them. He jerked his head toward a drawer in the corner. "Silverware is in there."

She rose and retrieved forks and laid them on the table. "I don't suppose we have any napkins."

"No such luck, although there are some small towels in that cabinet."

They sat down, and he waited while she bowed her head to pray, her lips moving silently. His shoulders slumped as the muscles relaxed. A quiet morning over breakfast. Nothing he'd ever needed before, but today was different. After the danger of the last two days, an intimate meal for two felt right…almost healing. What would it be like to wake up every day to a woman like Emily?

A lock of hair tumbled across her cheek, and his breath caught. He clasped his hands to prevent himself from tucking the silky-looking strand behind her ear. Warning bells rang in his head. If he didn't rein in his emotions toward his beautiful partner, the Germans were going to be the least of his troubles.

Chapter Nine

Needles of pain shot through Emily's back. She'd fallen asleep on the sofa after breakfast, and the lumpy cushions had done nothing to support her body. She massaged the muscles around her kidneys and winced. Rotating her neck, she rubbed her shoulders.

"Hey, sleepyhead. You're finally awake." Gerard stood in the doorway to the kitchen, a towel tossed over his shoulder. "While you snored, I washed the dishes and checked supplies. Not much here, but it should keep us in good stead for a few days before we shop."

Her face heated. "I didn't snore. Did I?"

"Not too loudly." He shook his head and chuckled. "Kidding. You didn't make a peep."

He winked, and she ducked her head to peer at her watch. Three hours had passed since she agreed to get some shut-eye in preparation for the rest of their day. She pulled on the band holding her hair in a ponytail, then finger-combed her tangled strands. She must look like bride of Frankenstein's monster. "Where's the powder room? I'd like to freshen up."

"Down the hall, second door on the right. Don't take too long. We need to review our plans."

She rose, hitched up her slacks, and smoothed her shirt. Executing a mock salute, Emily sauntered out of the living room. She found the bathroom and shut the door. A pale, haggard version of her face stared at her from the mirror. After reforming a ponytail, she opened the faucet and filled her cupped hands with water, splashing the sleep from her eyes.

A tiny piece of soap perched on the edge of the sink. She grabbed it and turned on the water in the tub. Stripping off her clothes, she lowered herself and sighed. The cool liquid brought tingles to her muscles.

*Thank You, Father, for providing a bathroom with running water. I'll never take modern plumbing for granted again.* She hummed her favorite hymn as she lathered up, then rinsed off. Footsteps sounded in the hallway then muffled bumps and bangs. More reconnaissance?

Gerard's face sprang to mind. Why hadn't he looked bedraggled and weary? Instead, he appeared rested and ready for the day. Maybe he'd bathed while she snoozed. No, he'd promised to keep watch. The army must provide a class on how to look neat and refreshed after an all-night hike and no sleep. He'd obviously passed with flying colors.

She giggled then clamped her teeth over her lips. This was a mission, not a date, although the two of them alone in the house created an intimacy she'd not expected.

Emily let out the water and toweled off, then slapped her forehead. She'd been in such a rush to clean up, she'd forgotten her satchel. Reaching for her discarded outfit and using it as a cover, she peeked out the bathroom door and caught sight of her bag propped against the jamb.

Gerard had anticipated her needs. She dragged on the clothes, her muscles protesting. "That man is an enigma. One minute forceful and obnoxious, the next thoughtful and solicitous."

Like no one she'd ever known. She'd rarely dated, but the boys she'd stepped out with seemed two dimensional and dull compared to Gerard. Quick witted, his humor was razor sharp and at times self-deprecating. His eyes missed nothing, and he seemed to process situations with lightning speed. She couldn't ask for a better partner. If she lived through the mission, her survival would be because of him, not anything she did.

Emily brushed her hair and studied her reflection. The puffiness on her lids remained, but the redness had disappeared. Somewhat bloodshot, her eyes still held vestiges of fatigue. She rummaged through the bag until she found her toothbrush and powder.

She needed to be convincing as a blushing bride, but she'd never been good as a simpering female. Would the townspeople believe their charade?

Since arriving, he'd been nothing like the overbearing dictator-instructor who'd drilled her during the last three months. He'd fed her, tucked her in, and then taken care of the house. What would it be like to be his wife for real?

Her face flushed, and Emily looked away from the glass. She balled up her dirty clothes and grabbed the handle of her valise. She opened the door and made her way to the bedroom where she stashed her things in the closet.

Rule number one: Never get romantically involved with your partner.

She rubbed the back of her neck. How was she supposed to remain detached when HQ had paired them as a married couple? They'd hold hands, his strong, calloused palm cradling hers. Would Gerard kiss her, stroke her hair, or put his arm around her like any normal man in love?

What would it be like to have his lips on hers or his fingers threaded through her hair? To be wrapped in his embrace? A shiver crawled up her spine. It would be breathtaking. Of that she had no doubt.

She lifted her chin. College drama club was in the past, but she'd give a performance worthy of an Academy Award, and no one would be the wiser. Only she would know he was beginning to edge his way into her heart.

---

Gerard sat at the scarred wooden table and studied the map. He'd already committed it to memory, but contemplating the scrap of silk might take his mind off the proximity of his partner during her morning ablutions.

The door opened down the hall, and moments later Emily appeared in the kitchen. Her hair hung down her back in a wet rope, her face glowed from scrubbing. She'd changed into a simple white, buttoned-down shirt and black pants. He glanced at her bare feet, slender with nails trimmed short and painted a light pink. He'd never figured her for a nail-polish girl. She continued to surprise him.

She dropped into the nearest chair. "What are your plans for the day? Have you figured out how to make contact with any of the Resistance cells?"

He shrugged. "First, let's figure out the best place to hide your radio. We should have done that first thing this morning. I'm getting sloppy, and that won't do."

"Is pulling up one of the floorboards too obvious?"

"Yes, but hiding it in the open, so to speak, may be the best idea."

"It's been two years since the Germans arrived. These people must be worn down from fear and looking over their shoulders. How does the free zone manage to remain unoccupied?"

"The name is a bit of a misnomer. Technically, the zone is under Vichy rule, but for some reason Marshal Pétain administers the laws in the south in an unrestricted fashion, rather than the strict way he does so in the north. I'm not sure how much longer Hitler will allow the demarcation to occur. He won't stop until he's swallowed all of Europe and more."

Emily shuddered. "He is a madman, but from what I understand, he created a sense of pride within Germany, so that many have chosen to overlook his actions."

"I find it hard to believe that everyone in the German army follows his rhetoric or that of the Nazis. As in our own country, military service is mandated. What is it like to put your life on the line for a cause you don't support?"

"That would be awful, wouldn't it? Young men who want to hold a job and raise a family being forced to carry a gun and go to war." She shook her head. "Will you apply for work at the factory immediately?"

"I'll hold off with that for a bit while I get the lay of the land." He reached into his pocket and withdrew a patch that he placed over one eye then strapped around his head. Slouching, he put his right foot at a forty-five-degree angle and limped around the kitchen, dragging the affected limb. "No one wants a cripple."

Her eyes widened. "Amazing. Your whole persona changed. But you must be careful. Hitler gets rid of those he deems a blight on society."

"Exactly why I should find a job and contribute to the cause, although it will pain me to do so."

"Can you sabotage your work in some way?"

"Maybe. I'll have to see how exacting they are with their quality control procedures." He waggled his eyebrows. "I might be able to put a wrench in the works."

"Ugh. Very punny."

He snickered. "As I said, employment may be a last resort, especially if I connect with a local cell that can keep me…ah…busy with mischief." He cocked his head. "Do you feel up to going to the market? It's a bit late, but shopping is a good way to start conversations with the locals. Don't be too inquisitive at this early stage, but sprinkle our cover story into the community. Find out the identity of the village busybody."

"I can do that but should wait for a bit until my hair dries. We may not be in high society, but no proper woman leaves the house with wet hair." She flipped her damp strands then reached for the map. "We should probably hide this, too."

The scent of her soap wafted past his nose, and his jaw clenched. Hopefully, they wouldn't have to go into the village often where he'd have to cling to her like a new husband. That kind of regular proximity could create chinks in his armor, although if Emily was as smart as he thought, she'd give him wide berth. No woman in her right mind would saddle herself with him. Jaded and imperfect, damaged goods, in all honesty, he'd make a terrible mate. She deserved a steady, all-American boy who came from a solid family. Not some guy from an immigrant family who had to earn his U.S. citizenship rather than be born to it. Sure, he went to college, but he'd barely graduated and almost been expelled twice. Why did he always seem to make poor choices?

No, Emily Strealer was out of his league.

Too bad he couldn't get his heart to agree.

## Chapter Ten

Emily shifted the willow basket on her arm and poked a shriveled turnip on display in the village market. She sighed and selected two. They'd been at the house for a week, and she was already tired of the fleshy root vegetable. *Forgive my ungratefulness, Lord. I'm like the Israelites who complained about manna. At least You have provided, and we will not starve. Thank You for Your blessings.*

She glanced at Gerard who'd accompanied her. The patch over his eye gave him a roguish air and made him even more handsome, as if that were even possible. He'd spent hours outside doing mischief, as he called it, and his skin had darkened to bronze contrasting with his dark hair and ice-blue eyes.

They moved to the next booth, and she frowned. More turnips. She picked up another one and brightened at the sight of some potatoes nestled in the bottom of the box. Firm and medium-sized, they set her mouth to watering. How life had changed. At home, she never gave food a thought, and now she was salivating over a root vegetable. After paying for four potatoes, she smiled. She would make her grandmother's latke recipe for dinner.

A young woman of perhaps high school age raced into the square, face flushed, and blonde hair escaping from the bun on her head. "The Germans are coming. There are two of them, and I heard them say they know there is a radio broadcasting from our village." She waved her arms. "They will search until they find the person responsible."

Emily gasped then clamped her teeth over her lips. Her heart pounded. "We must go. I failed to put away the radio after last night's transmission," she hissed in Gerard's ear.

He took the basket from her and grabbed her arm, his eyes glittering with anger. "You go ahead. It will blow my cover if I can suddenly rush home on two good legs. I won't be far behind you."

She nodded and quick-walked to the tiny house three blocks away. With trembling fingers, she pried up the floorboards under the kitchen table. She dismantled the radio equipment and shoved it into the cramped space before putting the boards back in place. She rushed outside and grabbed a handful of dirt. Returning to the house, she sprinkled the soil in several locations, then retrieved a broom and began to sweep.

Footsteps clomped on the front porch. She pressed a hand to her throat. *Please, God, let it be Gerard.*

The door swung open, and he stood on the threshold, hair and clothing disheveled, his eye wide as his gaze ricocheted around the room. "It's hidden, then?"

"Yes, and I've made a mess on the floor in the hope they'll not notice anything amiss with the boards."

"Atta girl. Good thinking."

His words warmed her, and she squared her shoulders. "We'll be ready. Not putting away the radio was foolhardy."

"A mistake, to be sure, but we took care of the situation. Now, we wait. How about if we start cooking to appear nonchalant."

"I don't know that I can eat anything." Emily pressed a hand against her middle where a swarm of bumblebees seemed to have taken up residence.

"Nerves are normal, but it's what you do with them that makes the difference. One step at a time. Cook first, then offer some to our *visitors.* Again, giving the appearance that we're no threat of subterfuge."

She took a deep breath. Time to prove she could be an effective agent. She rummaged in the cabinets and pulled out a large bowl. Digging in the drawers she found a paring knife and wooden spoon.

Gerard closed the door and set the basket on the table. He enveloped her in a hug and placed a kiss on her forehead before releasing her. Bending so his gaze was even with hers, he grasped her arms. "You are a strong, capable woman. Cooking may not be your forte, but acting is, so knock 'em dead, Vivien Leigh."

Her breathing ragged, she giggled. He'd kissed her. If he thought to calm her, he was mistaken. The feel of his warm lips and firm hands remained on her skin, tingling. She fought the urge to look in the mirror to see if there was evidence of his caress.

Snatching an apron from the hook on the wall, she wrapped it around herself then grabbed one of the potatoes from the basket and pared the skin from the fleshy bulb. If she didn't slash her fingers or stab her palm, it would be a miracle. She closed her eyes for a long moment. *Lord, our lives depend on my abilities here, but without You, I'm nothing, helpless to do my part. Please give me peace in these circumstances, but whatever happens, I'll know it's Your will.*

She opened her eyes.

Gerard stared at her, his face impassive. "Praying again, are you?" His voice held no emotion.

"Yes, and it would do you well to pray, too."

"Perhaps, but I'll rely on my skills and abilities at this point."

"Suit yourself."

Shouts rang out in the street.

Emily's stomach roiled, threatening to spill its meager contents. She swallowed then licked her lips. Her knees quavered, so she yanked out the chair and dropped onto the rickety seat. She gripped the potato and continued to peel.

Heavy pounding rattled the door on its hinges. *"Öffne die Tür!"*

She lifted her chin and gave Gerard a curt nod. *"Un moment."*

Wiping her hands on her apron, she crossed the room and turned the knob.

Two lanky men towered over her, their mouths twisted in snarls. One wore a gestapo uniform, the other the attire of a Vichy policeman.

"We have reason to believe you are hiding a radio. We will find it, and you will be arrested."

"We…we have nothing like that here, sirs. We are simple folks, but you are welcome to search our home." She stepped back.

They marched into the house, their necks swiveling as their gazes swept back and forth.

She ducked her head to hide her smile. There was nothing funny about their presence, but they looked like a pair of puppets connected by the same string. "Do you mind if I continue to prepare lunch?"

The German glowered. "*Nein.* You will stand against the wall and wait." He motioned to Gerard. "You, too."

Gerard rose with seeming difficulty, his neck and back bowed. He shuffled to Emily's side, his leg dragging in an uneven gait.

"You're pathetic. What happened to you?"

"An accident at work last year. A machine misfired…took my eye and broke my leg in four places. Your doctors considered amputating it, but they were able to save it. I worked at a munitions factory…for the führer. They shipped me home after I healed."

"You are lucky it happened in Germany. Our physicians are the best in the world. Elsewhere, you would have lost the limb."

"Yes, sir."

Emily reached over and clasped Gerard's hand, her heart pounding. "We married shortly after he came home."

The man smirked. "Ah, newlyweds. How fortunate for you this woman was willing to settle for a less than perfect man."

Gerard wrapped his arm around her shoulder. "I am indeed blessed. We have known each other since childhood."

"You are lucky someone would have you. The Frau obviously doesn't mind not having children."

The shorter man narrowed his eyes. "I know you, don't I?"

She shook her head. "Non. How could you? I have never left the village."

"You are lying. My name is Phillippe Caron, and we were at university together."

Her palms slicked, and Gerard squeezed her hand in silent support.

"I didn't attend college. My family had no money for that." Could he hear the tremble in her voice?

Caron stepped forward, inches from her. He leaned down, his nose a hairsbreadth from hers. "You can continue to deny it, but the fact is, you are not telling the truth. You are that American *mademoiselle* who spent two terms at university. I know because I could never forget that face. You may not remember me, but I certainly remember you."

His partner strode toward her. He grabbed a fistful of her hair and yanked her head backward. "Is this true? Are you an American?"

Emily cried out, her eyes squeezed shut against the pain. Her scalped burned.

Gerard rose up and swung at the man, but Caron caught his punch and shoved him to the floor. He fell with a grunt. "Leave my wife alone. She is not who you say. We are poor people who mind our own business."

"Are you calling me stupid? I recognize this woman. She may be your wife, but I doubt it. She is the American I knew at school. I watched her every day. I was a sniveling schoolboy at the time, without the nerve to ask her out, but now I am a man…a man with the power to let her live…or not."

"Please…you're hurting me." Emily wrapped her hands around the soldier's arm who continued to grip her hair. Would their mission fail because of an unrequited crush she knew nothing about? She truly didn't remember Caron, but he had recognized her. Her math skills were poor, but the odds of a schoolmate from ten years ago arriving in a tiny French village had to be astronomical. *Really, Lord. What is Your plan with this?*

Caron laid his hand on the man's shoulder. "*Monsieur* Krause, please release her. You gestapo are too rough for my taste."

Krause glared at Caron. "*Sturmbannführer,* and this is my interrogation. You are here as a representative of the French government, but I did not have to allow you to accompany me. I could have brought one of my officers."

"Understood." He leered at Emily then stroked her cheek. "But when you are finished questioning her, I would like some time with the woman, and I'd rather she wasn't damaged. I will show her what it's like to be with a real man, not this pitiful excuse."

Emily gasped, and Gerard scrambled to his feet, his hands clenched.

Caron laughed and pulled out his gun, his mouth twisted. "Suddenly, you can walk?"

Krause shoved Emily toward Gerard and withdrew his weapon. "Perhaps you are correct, after all, Caron. We have found the spies." He yanked off Gerard's eyepatch and tossed it on the floor. "*Lieber Gott.* Your eye is not missing. It is a miracle."

"I didn't mean I'd literally lost the eye. I meant my vision." Gerard scowled. "We are telling the truth."

Krause slapped Gerard. "No, you are not. We will take all the time we need to get the answers we are looking for. It seems you care for this woman at some level, so perhaps if we threaten her safety, you will answer our questions."

Emily clenched her fists, her fingernails biting into her palms. Perspiration trickled between her shoulder blades as the two men verbally sparred. The situation was escalating. Would she and Gerard get out alive?

Gerard snorted a harsh laugh. "You Germans think you are the master race, yet your tactics involve intimidating a woman. What man does that? You are nothing but a bully trying to prove he is a man. You have failed."

With a roar, Krause raised his arm and struck Gerard with the butt of his pistol. "I should kill you where you stand."

Stumbling but remaining on his feet, Gerard lowered his head and charged his attacker. They fell to the ground, and the gun skidded across the floor.

Caron pointed his weapon at the two men, the barrel wavering.

Emily watched the fight, her eyes wide and her lips trembling. Should she try to disarm Caron? She didn't want to make matters worse. She peeked at him in her peripheral vision. He seemed intent on the combatants rather than her. Could she get his gun?

The men climbed to their feet, and Gerard punched Krause, temporarily stunning the man.

Krause growled and stretched out his arm toward the discarded weapon, his fingers scrabbling on the floor. Closer. Closer. His palm wrapped around the grip, and he turned the gun toward Gerard.

A scream tore from Emily's throat.

Panting and grunting, Gerard grabbed Krause's arm and shoved it away. The weapon discharged, and Caron clutched his chest, his eyes clouding. He faltered, his pistol tumbling from his grasp. He took one step then a second before falling to his knees. A bubbling gasp escaped his mouth, and he pitched forward, coming to rest in silence.

Nausea swept over Emily. No training in the world prepared her for the horrific realities of a violent death. She pressed a hand to her mouth. She could not be sick. Not now. Not here.

Krause's face darkened, and he swung the gun toward Gerard again. He pulled the trigger.

Click.

The pistol didn't fire.

He tossed it away and grabbed Gerard around the throat.

Emily sprang into action. She had to save Gerard. She was an agent, not a sniveling female. Her gaze ricocheted around the room before coming to rest on the rolling pin. She rushed to the table and picked up her weapon.

Racing to the men, she swung at Krause striking the back of his skull. Stunned, his grip on Gerard loosened, and he slumped over.

Was he dead? Emily's stomach roiled.

Gerard flung off the limp German and stood. "Well done. We must tie him up and get out of here before he comes to."

Emily nodded. The man lived. She pulled open a kitchen drawer and retrieved a stack of old dish towels. With the paring knife, she tore them into strips as she went back to the living room, avoiding a glance at the body of the dead Frenchman.

Gerard had already wrestled the soldier into one of the kitchen chairs. The man's head lolled to one side, his face ashen. Pulling Krause's arms behind the chair, Gerard tied his wrists together then restrained the man's upper arms and ankles. "That should hold him for a while."

"You didn't kill him."

"No. And we may regret that decision, but my conscience will not let me shoot the man in cold blood. It would be murder."

She gaped at him, her heart full at his mercy toward the enemy soldier. "You know he would kill you if the situation were reversed."

"I've no doubt you're right, and I may not be on speaking terms with God at the moment, but I'm not interested in breaking His sixth commandment." He jerked his head toward the bedroom. "Go pack our things, and I'll retrieve the radio. The sooner we get out of here, the better."

"That is correct."

Emily's head whipped toward the German whose eyes were now open, his expression haughty.

"Flee now, but you won't get far. You will be found, and when that happens, you will die."

Chapter Eleven

Emily's thighs burned as she pedaled the rickety bicycle up and down the hills of the French countryside. Behind her, Gerard's breathing was labored. He hadn't complained, but his head had to be throbbing after the blow from the German. Hours had passed since they fled the small house with their few belongings and the radio.

Shadows lengthened in the setting sun. Darkness would soon cover them.

Perspiration sealed her blouse to her skin, yet the breeze chilled her, and she shivered. How could she be cold and overheated at the same time? Her slick palms sought purchase on the handlebars as she ascended another incline. If she wasn't running for her life, she might actually enjoy the pristine views of vineyards and villas.

The pedals lost traction, and she looked down. The chain had slipped off the cog. She heaved a sigh then steered her bike to the side of the road. Dragging her right foot, she slowed the vehicle then jumped off the seat and stopped.

Gerard pulled up beside her. "Is everything all right?"

"The chain may be broken."

"Let's take a look." He laid his bike on the ground then grabbed hers and turned it upside down. He examined the crank arm and ran his finger along the chain. Brow furrowed, he tugged on the metal links. Several grunts later, he looked up with a smile. "All fixed. Who knows the last time these poor bikes were greased. We're lucky they've carried us this far." He flipped the bike upright, and she took it from him.

Emily glanced down the road. "How much farther should we ride before holing up for the night?"

He dug into the inner pocket of his jacket and withdrew the handkerchief-sized silk map. He held it toward the dimming sun then poked at the thick, twisted line that ran through the center of the material. "I suggest we put in at least another fifty miles. I'd like us to make it as far as Provins. There's a small Resistance cell that operates out of that village."

"Fifty miles." Emily's shoulders sagged. Did she have the stamina for the distance? She had to. Once the German soldier was discovered, his troops would pursue them using gasoline-powered vehicles that ate up miles like starving locusts.

"You can do it. I know you're exhausted, but we'll take breaks."

"I'll pray for strength. Our lives depend on it." She ran her hand through her hair. "We need to consider new disguises, don't we? You've removed the eyepatch, and a limp isn't obvious unless you're walking, but anyone who sees us will wonder why a strapping man such as yourself isn't in uniform."

He puffed out his chest and grinned. "Strapping, am I?"

She giggled. "Thanks for lightening the mood. Even with all the lectures and book reading, I wasn't prepared for the emotional and physical reactions to the fear of being caught. My brain is racing, and my adrenaline must be off the charts. Every nerve in my body seems to be standing on edge."

With a sober smile, he nodded. "All normal reflexes. You can't really know what it's like until you've experienced the terror. But you're doing great. I'm proud to be your partner."

Her face warmed. For a man not prone to handing out compliments, he sure knew how to give one. She held up a lock of hair. "I should cut then dye my hair. Blonde, I think. Hopefully, we can get our hands on some peroxide."

"A blonde, huh? That will be interesting to see. Perhaps, the Resistance has a supply. They must have to constantly change their appearances. And maybe I'll lighten my hair as well."

"It might be better to find something to turn it gray." She tilted her head. "And you should grow a beard or mustache. They won't be looking for that, will they?"

"Good idea." He rotated his neck and rubbed his forehead before stuffing the map into its hidden pocket. "Let's ride for another thirty minutes. Think you can do that?"

"Yes, but you have a headache, don't you?"

He shrugged. "That German packed a good wallop. I've got a goose egg on the side of my head. Will probably bruise if it hasn't already."

"You should see a doctor."

"Not a chance. I'll be fine. We can't risk seeing too many people, especially those in positions of authority. Who knows how many physicians are on the Nazi payroll?"

"Understood." She squeezed his forearm. "Thanks for what you did in the cottage. You saved us."

"It was them or us, wasn't it?" Gerard frowned. "We may regret not killing the French gestapo agent. They're a ruthless bunch, without mercy. They'll see my actions as weak."

"Then they will have underestimated you. The world doesn't understand mercy and grace. Whether you believe it or not, you acted with the Holy Spirit's leading. I agree with you that killing that man outright would have been murder. You subdued him, and we were able to get away. It takes a big man to make that sort of decision." She pressed her lips together. "Besides, it's my fault we were compromised. I did know the Frenchman. He was right. We were in college together."

"You can't take the blame for that. France is nearly the size of Texas. What are the odds you'd run into a schoolmate?"

"Apparently, better than we realized."

---

Gerard chuckled at the sarcasm that dripped from Emily's words. "Too bad I'm not a gambling man." He motioned to her bike. "We've rested long enough. Let's get going."

Climbing on his bike, he winced as his vision swirled. If he was someone who liked to bet, he'd wager he had a concussion. No need to pass that tidbit along to Emily. She'd make them stop for the night, and there was no way he was going to allow them to spend hours outdoors. Another risky long shot.

Evening fell, and they continued to pedal. Dizziness threatened to overtake him, but he pushed himself to keep moving. *Please, God, provide us with somewhere to hide. Neither of us is in good shape, and we're only going to get more tired. I have no right to ask You, but please do it for Emily. She's one of Your children and deserves Your help.* He shook his head then groaned as his eyesight swam. Would God listen to a wayward rogue who'd turned his back too many years ago to count?

Minutes later, a small house appeared on their left. Farther down the road, several houses clustered on either side of the street. Gerard blinked. Had God conjured up a village in response to his prayer, or was this a real place? By his calculations, they should not have arrived at Provins yet.

The door to the building swung open, and Gerard froze. Had they come this far only to be discovered by the occupying forces? His grip tightened on the handlebars. He could sense Emily's taut frame behind him.

A bent figure shuffled to the edge of the porch. "Come inside. I've been waiting for you." A raspy, smoke-filled voice drifted toward them. "Hurry. The patrols will soon begin."

"Is it safe?" Emily barely spoke above a whisper.

"Only if God answers a sinner's request. I just prayed for safe haven, and the house appeared. I don't know what to think."

Her teeth flashed white in the darkness. "We're all sinners, Gerard. If your plea is honest, He will respond. I believe He's showing that He still cares for you."

"Then why hasn't He rescued the Jews and other persecuted folks?"

"Men more knowledgeable than I have debated that question for decades. Let's step forward in faith and enter the house."

"Shh. Stop talking and wheel your bikes inside. If they are left outside, the soldiers may requisition them, or worse, decide my home is worth searching."

"Wait here." Gerard wrestled his bicycle up the steps and through the open door then returned to carry Emily's into the house. The door closed behind them, and a light sprang on with a click.

He squinted against the illumination as his eyes protested.

Their host was an elderly woman with bright blue eyes set among the sea of wrinkles that lined her face. Iron-gray hair was pulled back in a bun at the base of her neck, and she wore a faded floral housedress. Scuffed boots covered her feet.

"Welcome to my home. Please be seated, and I will bring you refreshments. Then we can get down to the business of hiding you."

"What—" Gerard gaped at her retreating back then turned to Emily. "Who is this woman, and how did she know we were coming?"

"You said it yourself. You prayed for shelter."

"So…what…God told her we were coming?"

"Possibly. We'll have to wait and see what she says. But God is still in the miracle business, and she may be close enough to Him that He speaks directly to her. Don't lose your fledgling faith so soon."

The woman returned from the kitchen carrying a tray that held a teapot, three cups, and a plate full of cheese sandwiches. "You must be hungry after your journey. Eat up."

Gerard sprang forward, his mouth watering at the tangy aroma of the cheese, and took her burden, setting it on a low table in the living room. He guided Emily to a nearby seat then waited for the old woman to select a chair before lowering himself onto the sofa. "Thanks for your generosity."

She dipped her head in acknowledgment then reached for their hands. "Let's thank God for His bounty. Then we can chat."

His mind reeled. Perhaps Emily was right, and the Lord had directed this woman to take care of them. She seemed to be in close contact with Him.

"Dear Father, thank You for sending these young people to me. Guide our actions, and keep us safe through the night. Give us all our much-needed sleep, and help us arise in the morning, fresh and ready to greet the day. Bless this food for our bodies. Please give us the strength to do Your bidding. Amen."

She looked up with a smile. "I will not ask your names nor will I give you mine. I'm sure you understand."

"Absolutely." Gerard lifted a sandwich and took a bite, trying not to wolf down the tender bread and cheese combination. "We are grateful for the food. Our last meal was a long time ago."

"That is often the case with my…uh…guests. You have ridden many miles, oui?"

"You're part of the—"

She held up a hand. "I am a loyal French citizen who is troubled by what she sees happening in her dear country." She cocked her head. "The Nazis seek you?"

He nodded. "Yes. We're headed to…well…farther from here, but first we must change our appearance. Do you have scissors and peroxide?"

"Of course." Her lips twitched, and a raspy laugh filled the room. "What good French woman doesn't? Finish your meal while I get what you need." She toddled back to the kitchen, and Gerard glanced at Emily who wore a bemused smile.

"I've known God all my life and heard of special times like this, but it has never happened to me." She pulled the band from her ponytail, and her hair swung free. "You'll need to cut my hair. I can't reach the back."

Gerard swallowed. What would it be like to run his hands through the shimmering strands? "I'm not exactly skilled in the art of hairdressing. You may want our friend here to do the deed."

She grinned. "Nonsense. Just cut it one length even with my chin. Then we'll dye it, Jean Harlow style."

"If you insist."

"I do." Emily leaned forward and laid her hand on his arm, the warmth of her fingers penetrating his shirt. "Gerard, I have peace about the situation. We are safe, at least for the moment. Tomorrow is another day. In the meantime, let's enjoy the sanctuary we have."

"I wish I had your faith."

"Look inside. You may be surprised to find you have more than you think."

"It's been a long time since I've had a real relationship with God. Do I really deserve His protection?"

Chapter Twelve

Emily yawned and stretched, her back protesting from the movement. She swung her bare feet out of the hard bed. Their new location was rustic at best, but at least they were safe for the time being.

They'd stayed a day with the mysterious French woman who most assuredly had been sent by God. While there, she regaled them about her experience of hearing His voice during her prayers telling her to go outside and hide whomever was in the yard. She insisted she was not of the Resistance but simply following instructions from her Lord.

Skeptical, Gerard had been jumpy during their entire stay. But there seemed to be no other explanation than a miracle as to how she would have heard them in the darkness and then offered them sanctuary. Emily shook her head. If she lived to return to America, she would tell everyone about the extraordinary event. Well, as long as it didn't conflict with her vow of secrecy.

Under cover of darkness, they'd been picked up by another French woman, this one a Resistance member who agreed to pass them through the network to the border. Gerard found her after a long night of guarded conversations with the barkeep at a small pub. She drove them in a rattletrap car to a tiny cottage into the village. Four days had passed since their arrival, and two days since Gerard slipped out the front door claiming he'd be back soon.

His new disguise suited him. If possible, he was even more handsome than when they first met. He'd shaved his head, and the two-day growth on his jaw lent an air of piracy to his countenance. His blue eyes flashed whenever Emily and he were together. His jaw seemed permanently set in determination.

Noise sounded from below. Had he returned?

She rose and grabbed her borrowed clothes from the back of a chair. Dressing hurriedly, she caught sight of her reflection in the mirror above the bureau and blinked. Would she ever get used to herself as a blonde? Emily fingered a lock of hair, dry and brittle, and sighed. So much for her Jean Harlow look. More like a clown.

More bangs and bumps under her feet. She slipped on her boots and strode from the room to make a quick trip to the bathroom to wash her face and brush her teeth. After clomping down the stairs to the kitchen, she stopped in the doorway.

No Gerard. Her heart fell. Was he still alive, or had he been caught? Would she ever see him again?

Francoise, or whatever her real name was, stood in front of the stove stirring a pot of oatmeal. A skillet of scrambled eggs sat on the counter. She jerked her head to the loaf of bread. "Please cut a couple of slices. Breakfast is ready."

"Where did you manage to get eggs?"

"A small basket of food was left on the back stoop this morning. Apparently, someone decided to share from their bounty. Perhaps your *petit ami*?" Her left eyebrow rose as she cocked her head.

"He's not my boyfriend." Her cheeks warmed.

"Your red face belies your words." Francoise dished out their food then picked up her plate and bowl. She sat at the table and began to spoon the porridge into her mouth. "Sit. Eat. I received a message that you must relay."

Emily's head shot up. "Why did you let me sleep? Information must be sent as soon as it arrives."

The woman's shoulder lifted in a careless shrug. "There is no need for alarm. It came only a few minutes ago." She pushed a slip of paper across the table and continued to eat.

Emily coded the message then dragged out the radio and transmitted the secret missive.

Francoise laid down her fork. "After you've eaten, we'll head to the market. There's little food in the house, and with any luck we'll hear something of value. You'd be surprised at how loose-lipped my fellow citizens are."

"At home, the government issues posters about that. They were everywhere. Bus and subway stations, groceries stores, just about anywhere you looked."

"It's hardly the same situation. Saying the wrong thing here can get you killed. Not likely to happen in America."

"Perhaps not in the U.S., but something said there could be conveyed over here. If this war has taught me nothing else, it is how small the world is. The incident at the farmhouse is a prime example. Thousands of troops, and I run into a fellow college student."

"You Americans have had it easy in this war. Oui, you've lost troops, but your forces are only here because the Japanese dragged you into the conflict. There are many of your people who don't want to be part of this conflict. You can't possibly understand what is like for us. Pearl Harbor is nothing compared to the death and destruction in France since the Germans arrived."

Emily bit the inside of her lip. Truth be told, the woman was right. The Depression had been difficult for many in the U.S., and she'd been old enough to see the impact on schoolmates, but personally, her family had not suffered. And America was not being run roughshod over by a ruthless army. "Then tell me. Help me understand."

Francoise narrowed her eyes. "Why do you want to know?"

"Because it is important to you."

"What?"

"Look, I hear the bitterness in your voice because the struggle has been long and grueling, and the French must feel abandoned, but I don't have to experience the hardship to want to be part of the solution, to fight the evil that penetrated your country. I love France. I learned the language, studied here, and taught French and your culture to my students."

"I don't know if I can take you at your word about loving my country, however genuine you appear. Perhaps you are only here because of the attractive man who accompanied you."

Emily huffed and crossed her arms. "I am not here because of Gerard. He was my instructor, and our superiors deemed it necessary for us to pretend to be married. It makes no sense to me, but I follow orders."

Francoise winked. "You must admit, it is easy to profess to love someone so gorgeous."

"You think I would risk my life because of some man? How shallow do you believe me to be?"

"I have no idea."

"Then stop making assumptions. We don't have to be adversarial. We're on the same side." She frowned. "How about we focus on the mission?"

"Suit yourself."

*Show her grace, My child.*

Emily closed her eyes and sighed. Once again, her temper caused her mouth to run away with her words. Forgive me, Lord. She looked up at Francoise. "Whatever you think about my countrymen is your prerogative, but please know that I am here because I want to help France and her people get out from under Hitler's tyranny. I will do what I can to gain your confidence, but I understand if you choose to withhold your trust. Meanwhile, I'll continue to transmit messages and work with you however you need. Or I will stay in the house and out of sight." Emily rose and took her dishes to the sink. She turned on the spigot, cleaning the soiled plate and bowl. "Whichever you prefer."

"Unfortunately, I trust very few people." Francoise's voice was soft, uncertain.

"Understandable, but for the Resistance to succeed there must be some element of collaboration…er…bad choice of words, but you know what I mean."

"Oui."

"And Francoise?"

"Hmm?"

"Gerard is one of the most handsome men I've ever met, but if you ever tell him I said that, I'll claim you're lying. Are we clear?"

A laugh burst from Francoise's lips, and her eyes sparkled. "Very clear." She clapped her hands. "Ah, unrequited love. But, all is fair in love and war, so we shall see what happens."

"Francoise—"

The front door opened in the next room, and they froze, staring at each other, eyes wide. Footsteps clomped toward them, then Gerard appeared in the doorway, disheveled and dirty. Fatigue lined his face. His gaze swept the room. "Nice to see you ladies having a good time. What did I miss?"

Francoise tossed a look at Emily and chuckled. "You should ask your *éspouse,* but hurry, we're going out." She patted Gerard on the shoulder then slipped past him and out of the room.

He crossed his arms and raised his left eyebrow. His face flushed under the dust. "Wife?"

Emily's heart bumped in her chest. Clark Gable had nothing on Gerard. "She's keeping up the charade. Where have you been? I didn't realize you'd be gone so long."

"Now, who's keeping up the charade? Don't be a nagging wife." He sauntered to the sink and washed his hands. "Here and there, and my endeavors took longer than expected."

"You're not going to fill me in?"

"The less you know, the better." One shoulder lifted, but he didn't turn toward her.

"If we're going to be partners in this mission, I disagree."

"That's too bad. I'm the senior member, and I'll decide what information gets passed."

She strode to him and leaned forward so she could see his face, his overwhelmingly alluring face. He seemed determined to avoid her eyes. What was he hiding? Was he putting them in danger? Could she trust him with her life?

## Chapter Thirteen

Gerard dried the few dishes used during their meager dinner of fried eggs and potatoes. Emily cooked, so he offered to clean up. Night was falling outside, and his reflection stared back at him. Dark circles hung beneath his eyes. He hadn't slept well since they relocated three days ago to the outskirts of Paris. The small village was littered with German soldiers and gestapo.

He rotated his neck to ease the stiffness. The need to be closer to the action was crucial, but the possibility of being discovered drained him. A simple mistake could bring them to the attention of the authorities. Emily's transmissions might be detected. His stomach clenched, and his meal threatened to reappear.

His ears strained to pick up unusual sounds outside the house. Nothing.

Did he expect to hear a stealthy group intent on their capture?

"Are you okay?" Beside him, Emily's voice was soft, troubled. "You've sighed several times, and I doubt it has anything to do with your chore, unless you despise housework that badly."

"No. Just tense. My senses are on alert almost as if we're approaching a battle." He rubbed his burning eyes. "I'm constantly listening for noises that don't belong in the house."

She squeezed his arm then picked up the clean plates and returned them to the tiny cabinet over the stove. "We are on the front lines of battle, albeit near the streets of the capital rather than a hillside or beach. I can understand why you feel as you do." She smiled. "I'm glad you're on my side."

His arm tingled where she'd touched him, and he shook his head. Focus, Lucas. "How about another game of gin rummy? Maybe you'll beat me this time."

"Sure, but apparently beginner's luck is a fallacy." She grinned. "I haven't been able to win yet, and I've never played this game."

They walked to the small dining table, and Gerard held out one of the four tired-looking wooden chairs. The deck of cards remained on the table from their game the previous evening.

When she seated herself, the fresh scent of soap wafted from her hair, and he closed his eyes. His fingers itched to run through her shining tresses. How did she stay so spotless in their dingy surroundings? With his shaved head and the bristles on his jaw, he must look like a tramp. Yet, she'd been gracious and not said a word about his appearance.

She grabbed the cards and shuffled before dealing the appropriate number. Stacking the remainder, she picked up her hand and waved it with a grin, eyes flashing. "All right, *Major*, be prepared to lose."

Her face glowed, and he smiled. At least one of them was relaxed. "We'll see, *Miss Strealer*. I've been in tighter spots than this."

"I think I've got a chance tonight. Be prepared for some stiff competition."

"Of that I have no doubt." He snickered. "You seem to treat everything as a rivalry."

A shadow crossed her face, then she shrugged. "As the youngest, I was always trying to keep up with my sisters. Maybe it's different for boys, but we girls constantly tried to outdo each other." She picked up a card, studied her hand, then laid down the two of clubs. "Even childhood games became an opportunity to best one another."

"My brother and I were the same way." He nodded and tried to ignore the pang of grief that swept over him. "I don't have any sisters, and most women I've met seem…um…docile."

"Yeah, most of the gals I know are meek, but to be honest, it feels like society has expectations for us to be like that. Few women seem willing to go against the grain. Did you see some of the newspaper ads in America? Women are filling men's shoes in the workplace but are supposed to keep their hair, face, and nails done at the same time. Have you tried to maintain a manicure while welding or riveting?"

He selected a card, tucked it in his hand, and discarded. "Can't say that I have."

She giggled. "No, I guess not. But do you understand what I'm saying?"

His chest tightened at the earnest look on her beautiful face. Tension seemed to have drained from her, and they were just two people enjoying a night of leisure. Except for the fact the Nazis could break up their little party at any time. "I do. I hadn't thought about it until just now. I took it for granted that my mom is a strong woman as are her sisters. A formidable force, in fact. The three of them have championed several causes, raising funds, and getting legislation changed."

"Really? That's wonderful. My mom is all about propriety. Being with the right people, wearing the right clothes, doing the right things."

He cocked his head. "Right being…?"

Her expression hardened. "Fashionable, for lack of a better word. She wants all us girls to marry well into families of importance. Makes her sound rather shallow and callous, but I believe deep down she has our best interests at heart."

"That's generous. Most people wouldn't see past her actions."

"Mother didn't have much when she was growing up. Marrying my father changed everything for her. Perhaps she wants us to enjoy the same experience. But I don't need to marry to feel fulfilled. I don't want to risk being tied to a man who dictates my every move."

"Not all guys are overbearing."

"Why chance it?" She picked up a card, slid it into her hand, and put an unwanted card on the pile. "Despite the danger, I've never felt more alive. What I'm doing will make a difference in the long run. History may not remember my name, but it will be remember Americans came here to help wipe out the evil in this land."

"Your attitude would make you a good soldier. That's the sentiment most have. We're not seeking recognition, but we're driven to protect our country's way of life." He picked up a card, glanced at it, then laid it down. She had her heart set on winning. He'd wait for the four of diamonds. "Fascinating how being an agent doesn't seem much different."

She picked up the discarded four of spades and narrowed her eyes. "You're really going to let me win? I'm quite capable without your help."

"What?" He pinned what he hoped was a look of innocence on his face.

"I've been watching your moves, and I'm fairly certain you only needed one four to complete your hand. I may be new to the game, but you, of all people, know how high I scored on observation skills."

Gerard threw his head back and laughed. She was a smart one, and as usual he'd underestimated her.

Emily crossed her arms, her expression mulish. "Did you honestly think I'm dumb enough not to notice?"

"No, your intelligence has nothing to do with my actions. You wanted to win so badly, and I wanted to make it happen." He tossed his cards on the table. "Forgive me. I meant no harm. Let's start over, and I promise to allow you to beat me fair and square."

She wagged her index finger then pushed her cards toward him. "You better. Now, your turn to shuffle, and it's time for a change of topic. What were you doing before you joined the military?"

He fiddled with the cards to stall as his mind searched for innocuous information he could share. "Well, I'm half Canadian, and I attended the University of Montreal. Everyone in my family does. My brother and I were the fifth generation. No pressure there, huh? I majored in economics for my folks and political science for me. Did pretty good, too."

Her eyes widened. "I don't know why, but I hadn't figured you for a military man at heart."

"You figured right. I'd rather serve as an ambassador, an opportunity to study justice and liberty in countries around the world. To try to understand where their schools of thought came from in order to better work together."

"To go from spying on a country to working with them will be an interesting transition, don't you think?"

"Definitely."

"Do you have a preferred region you'd like to serve?"

He raked his fingers over his scalp, a habit he hadn't broken since shaving his head. "France."

"So, you would go from spying on them to collaborating."

"Yes, ambassador is a prime assignment. I'd have to work my way into the position. I'm willing to take what I'm given." He steepled his fingers. "What about you? Back to teaching after the war? You could do more with our experience."

"Except I can't tell anyone what I've done. Classified, remember?"

"Right, but you didn't answer my question."

She looked off into space, her brows furrowed in concentration.

Gerard willed himself not to rub out the wrinkle and have her turn those hazel eyes to him. He ran a finger around the inside of his collar. The night was becoming too cozy. All that was missing was a fireplace and wine. He needed to break the mood. Now. Who was he fooling? He was a military man, and he'd done things no respectable person did. She was beautiful, smart, and gracious, and in a different time and place, he'd try to win her over. But she deserved someone better than he could ever be. Someone who hadn't compromised his principles to win a war.

"Are you all right? You're flushed." She smirked. "Nervous about the rematch?"

"What? Uh…no." He stacked the cards then shoved back his chair and jumped to his feet. "But I'm no longer in the mood to play. I think I'll go outside and check the perimeter."

Her face fell. "Oh…uh…okay. Should we split up and share the reconnaissance?"

"No. Stay inside." His voice was harsh, and he winced when uncertainty then anger settled onto her face.

She rose. "Do you think I can't handle the task? We're in this together, or have you regressed into your damsel-rescuing-soldier self?"

He'd upset her again. What did he know about relationships? Good thing this one was fake. Wasn't it? "No. I just need some air. That's all, and I don't need help."

With a growl, he pivoted and marched out the door. He'd take the cowardly way out and remain on watch all night.

Chapter Fourteen

Emily jolted upright in the bed. She tugged aside the blackout curtain and sunlight streamed into the room. Her gaze shot to the nightstand, and she grabbed her watch. Five minutes after six. That wasn't possible. She held the timepiece to her ear and frowned. No ticking. In her anger at Gerard, she'd forgotten to wind it before retiring for the night. A rookie move if ever there was one.

She rolled her eyes and slapped her forehead. Gerard had every right to get testy with her. She continued to take one step forward and two steps back. Why on earth had she been selected? Did all the new agents make these kinds of errors?

With a deep breath, she swung her feet over the edge of the bed then closed her eyes. "Dear God, what have I gotten myself into? Is this really your plan for me? I know failing to wind my watch isn't a major mistake, but if I miss the small things, the big things are in danger of not succeeding. I don't want Gerard to lose his life because I messed up."

*Be strong and of good courage, fear not. I will not fail nor forsake thee.*

Warmth filled her, and tears sprang to Emily's eyes. She'd run ahead of the Lord again, and anxiety was the result, but He poured out His peace as soon as she'd asked. Would she ever learn to rest in Him, no matter what?

"Forgive my unbelief, Father. Help me trust in You today." She took a deep breath and changed clothes. She tucked her feet into her boots and clomped down the hall to the bathroom. A quick wash of her face and brush of her teeth, and she was ready to apologize to Gerard for last night's reaction. How would he take her words?

She pressed a hand against her stomach that buzzed as if a swarm of bumblebees had taken flight, then headed down the stairs and entered the kitchen.

Gerard sat at the table, his nose buried in *Le Temps*, one of Paris's most important newspapers that managed to remain in circulation even during the occupation, although the reliability of its content was debatable.

"There's a plate of ham and eggs warming in the oven. I thought you might be hungry."

Her stomach gurgled, and her face heated.

He chuckled. "Apparently, I thought correctly."

"Why did you let me sleep so long? The sun nearly blinded me when I opened the drapes."

"There's nothing on the schedule for the day as of yet. I'm reviewing the paper to see if there's anything of value to transmit. You obviously needed the rest."

She opened the oven door and pulled out the plate, the tantalizing aroma of the food tickling her nose. If he cooked her breakfast, maybe he was no longer angry with her. "Where on earth did you secure ham?"

"I went for a walk, and the generous farmer at the other end of the village gave me a small slab."

"I didn't think anyone had hogs left."

"Neither did I, but it's a long story, and suffice it to say I've been sworn to secrecy. Of course, now that we've partaken, we're complicit in the deed."

"Black market?"

"Probably, although I'm not sure how one hides a herd of pigs."

"That would be a challenge." She giggled then sobered. "Listen, about last night. I'm sorry I overreacted."

He shook his head. "No need to apologize. I was rather abrupt in my departure. I feel trapped in this house, and it makes me irascible. A bit like a bear with a sore paw. Not your fault."

"You're nice to say that, but I'm afraid it's my usual knee-jerk reaction of second-guessing myself and assuming you are, too. I continue to carry that into the job, the need to prove I'm capable and worthy." She shook her head. "Why didn't they pick that up during the psych evaluation?"

"I'm sure they did."

"Yet, they still gave me the assignment."

"Ours is not to reason why the quacks or higher-ups make the decisions they do." He shrugged. "They're paid a lot more money than we are, so let's pretend they know what they're about. Besides, a bit of healthy rivalry is a good thing, isn't it?"

"Says the man who lives as if every moment in life is a competition." She grinned to take the sting from her words then reached for the paper. "Anything in *Le Temps* worth sending out? We haven't transmitted for a couple of days."

"Yes." He poked at an article announcing a visit by *der führer* himself. "Apparently, he's decided a tour of the French countryside is in order. I'm stunned the Germans would allow the release of such information, especially with the assassination attempts in the past, but perhaps their arrogance makes them think they can keep him safe no matter what. We definitely need to pass this information along."

Her breath caught, and she laid down her fork. "Hitler's coming here? There will be even more soldiers and gestapo patrolling the area. Should we consider moving on?"

"Not yet. I want to gather more intelligence. In fact, the market today is sure to be reverberating with the news of Hitler's visit. Head to the square. Don't say much. Just listen. When you return, we'll glean fact from fiction before you transmit."

Emily nodded as she licked her lips. No longer hungry, she pushed away the plate still half filled with food. "I don't want to waste it, but—"

"Understood. You'll be great, and I'll be here when you return."

She pushed her chair from the table and stood. Opening a canister near the sink, she withdrew their ration book and several coins. "With any luck, I'll also get something for our supper." Her heart pounded in her ears. Could Gerard hear that? Why did she have to get skittish when leaving the house? Surely, other agents were also afraid.

Rising, Gerard folded the paper and tossed it on the table. He grasped her arms and bent to meet her eyes. "You are going to be fine. Nerves are normal. I'd be worried if you weren't apprehensive. As long as you don't let your feelings overwhelm you, the uneasiness will keep you alert." He pulled her into a quick embrace then placed a kiss on her forehead, his lips warm and dry. "Now, go get 'em, champ."

Her skin throbbed where he'd kissed her, and she stifled the urge to touch it. She studied his expression. Acceptance, encouragement, and another emotion she couldn't read, mingled on his handsome face. Her training kicked in, and she straightened her spine, lifted her chin, and tucked her hair behind her ears. She executed a mock salute and hurried from the kitchen, his chuckle following her out of the house.

She pressed a hand against her heart, skipping beats as if she and Gerard were in high school, and he'd just asked her to prom. Nothing could come of their relationship, if she could call it that. Farce was more like it, but he treated her like a colleague and friend. That was at least something. At home, she was the youngest teacher on staff, and most of her coworkers seemed tolerant of her presence. But here, she was an equal. Two agents on a mission. She took a deep breath. He was right.

Neither of them would be the same after the war. Could she go back to teaching high school students day in and day out? If she survived, would she prefer a mundane life rather than excitement and danger?

Her steps crunched on the road. She'd seen so much in her short time in France that she'd never be able to share with anyone. Greed. Cruelty. Starvation. The empty eyes of the oppressed who wondered whether they would ever regain their country's freedom. The desperate faces of those forced to make terrible decisions such as stealing, collaboration, or prostitution to feed their families. Would her family understand when she came home a different person?

Jostled from behind, she looked up. Villagers mingled with uniformed members of the Wehrmacht on the approach to the market. She hunched her shoulders and ducked her head, allowing her hair to shield most of her face. Slowing her pace to put her near a trio of older women, she fingered the coins in her pocket. Soldiers tended to gravitate toward single young women, probably seeing them as easy prey.

She nodded to the women, and one of them looped her hand through Emily's arm. "*Bonjour.* Shop with us this morning."

"*Merci.*" Emily sighed. Thank You, Lord, for sending protection, even if it is little old ladies.

They wended their way through the booths, prodding the pitiful-looking vegetables. What would they do over the winter when fresh produce wasn't available? She purchased a handful of potatoes and small turnips.

"We need to be rid of the Jews when der führer arrives."

Her ears pricked up. A quarter turn, and a senior gestapo officer came into view. Well over six feet tall, he towered above the junior officer. Blond, blue-eyed, and regal-looking, both epitomized Hitler's ideal German. She lowered her head.

"How many days do we have?"

"Three or four at the most, so we should begin immediately." Paper crackled as he withdrew a sheet from his inside pocket. "Start with this list, and I'll have another for you by tomorrow. These Jews and other undesirables think they can hide behind forged papers, fake marriages, and disguises, but we will find them."

"*Jawohl.*" The junior officer clicked his heels, saluted, and marched away.

Emily froze. When would the other man leave? He stood within inches, his riding crop tapping his thigh in a hypnotic rhythm. Sunlight gleamed on his polished boots, and without looking she knew his uniform was crisp and clean.

He turned and bumped into her. "Get out of my way, woman."

Her skin crawled as if spiders ran up her spine. "*Excusez moi.*"

Without a backward glance he strode away, and Emily blew out a deep breath. She leaned closed to the old woman. "I must return home. I…uh…feel faint. Can you walk with me?"

Her companion gave her a knowing look and nodded. She patted Emily's arm, then gestured to the other two women who waved.

They walked in silence for several yards, then the woman cleared her throat and pulled Emily forward. "We must move faster, and when you get home you must pack and leave. I saw a glint of interest in that gestapo man's eyes. He may have pushed you away, but he caught sight of your beauty. It may not be today or tomorrow, but you will open your door one day soon, and he will be there. And your husband won't have anything to say about it. The two of you should relocate to another village."

Emily's heart skittered, and she stumbled. Would she be the reason they were captured? Could she get the transmission sent before the officer arrived? They rushed forward, and moments later arrived at the house. "Would you like to come in?"

"Non. " The woman dipped her head. "You must go. Now. There is no time for dawdling." She squeezed Emily's hand and gave her the canvas bag that carried their purchases. "And may Almighty God go with you. I will pray for safe travels."

"Merci." For several seconds she watched the woman shuffle along the roadway.

Gerard appeared behind her. "Is everything all right?" His voice rumbled in his chest.

"No." She pointed to the retreating figure. "She thinks the gestapo officer who bumped into me will come for a visit. That I have peaked his interest. She suggests we clear out immediately." She trembled. "I'm sorry for compromising the mission."

His face darkened. "Nonsense. Do not take the blame for the fact that a man has noticed how attractive you are. Did you learn anything while at the market?"

"Yes." She relayed the conversation she'd heard. "We need to transmit right away. You pack, and I'll assemble the radio and send the message."

"Perhaps we should move and then send the information."

"Absolutely not. It is imperative that the Allies hear about Hitler's visit and the list of Jewish people. After you've pulled your things together, you should head out. I'll follow after I broadcast." She laid her hand on his arm. "Or perhaps we should split up."

A knock sounded on the door, and Emily jumped.

Gerard's head whipped up, and he stiffened.

She jerked her head toward the back of the house, and mouthed, "Go."

"I won't have you face this alone." His whisper caressed her cheek.

The rapping repeated. "Emily. It's Francoise. Open the door."

Emily yanked on the knob.

Francoise stood on the front step, her face red and perspiring. Her hair, normally pulled back in a severe bun, frizzed out around her face. She gripped her bicycle and gasped for air. "You must leave immediately."

"Yes, but how did you know about the man in the market?"

"What man?"

"The gestapo soldier."

"I know nothing about him. I'm here because you've been compromised. Somehow a list of agents is now in the hands of the Germans, and your name is on it. Both of you. You've been ordered back to England. Take your things and begin walking toward Rouen. When you arrive at Lyons-La-Forêt, go to the Café Éclair, and another agent will contact you with instructions for reaching the escape route out of France. The pass code phrase is 'All human wisdom is contained in two words: wait and hope.'"

"*The Count of Monte Cristo?*"

Francoise shrugged. "I don't make them up."

Emily bit her lip. "But I can't go. I must transmit the message."

"There is no time. If word reaches your gestapo officer, he and his men can be here in minutes. It's not safe for you to stay."

"But—"

Francoise held up her hand. "Don't argue. Give me the information, and I will see that it is sent, but you must leave right this moment. Is that clear?"

Gerard placed his hand on Emily's back, and she shivered at his touch. He shared the discussion Emily had heard in the marketplace with Francoise.

She nodded. "I will take care of it. Now go."

"Would you like some water?"

"There is no time. Good luck." She climbed onto her bike, wheeled it around, and pedaled down the street.

Emily swallowed. The moment she'd feared since landing in France had arrived. Would they make it out of the country alive?

Chapter Fifteen

The soles of Emily's feet burned, and her calves ached with each step. She shielded her eyes against the setting sun and trudged behind Tania, if that was her name, the woman leading them to freedom. It had been two days since leaving the cottage, and Tania was their fourth guide. They'd journeyed by foot or ridden in rattletrap trucks. Emily shifted the satchel from one shoulder to the other then stuffed her hands in her pockets. Gerard walked behind her, his stride steady and strong.

Tania was dressed as a nurse and carried papers signed by Stulpnagel himself, the German commander in Paris, giving them safe passage for humanitarian missions. The Resistance was bold if not creative.

Rustling sounded in the bushes, and Emily grabbed her chest. A squirrel raced across the road in front of her, its chatter strident. "Please, Lord, keep us safe."

She was jumping at shadows. Why couldn't she be as courageous as Gerard, whose impassive face had barely changed expression since leaving? His crystal-blue eyes glittered as they darted back and forth, his jaw squared. The battered fedora set low over his forehead shaded much of his face.

Stopping, Tania held up one hand then gestured toward the woods to their left. "Ça y est. From here we will follow a path that will lead you into the mountains. We have many more kilometers to go, and I will leave you at a way station where you will be met by another guide to take you on the next leg. The terrain will be difficult, so prepare yourself. *Prêt?* Are you ready?"

Emily hitched up her bag and nodded. Was she prepared? No. She wanted to toss the heavy pack onto the ground, lie on a bed that actually had a mattress, envelope herself under a goose-down comforter, and sleep for days. Would she let them know that? Not on her life.

Gerard spoke from behind. "Oui."

"Bon."

Tania held up a low branch. Emily and Gerard ducked underneath, foliage snapping under their boots. They trekked single file through centuries-old trees and bushes that tugged at their clothing.

Where was the trail? Emily's eyes burned as she strained to discern the invisible path. Her footfalls were muffled by the bed of pine needles and leaves that covered the forest floor. She tightened her grip on the walking stick Gerard had created for her on their first day. After hours of being held, the notches he'd carved for her hand were beginning to wear smooth.

Her breathing was ragged in her ears, and she pressed her lips together. She sounded like a TB patient. Tania would think her unable to complete the journey. Emily glanced behind, and her toe caught an unseen rock, pitching her toward the steep incline to her right. The staff flew from her hands, and her knees hit the ground, the weight of her pack pulling her onto the grassy slope.

Gravity took over, and she hurtled down the hill. Rolling. Rolling. Her hands reached out, fingers grasping for something…anything to halt her progress. Time seemed to freeze, and the sky tilted as her body continued its trajectory down the embankment, her limbs twisting and turning with her every rotation. Heat rushed through her body and coiled in her stomach. Nausea threatened then dissipated as quickly as it appeared.

She slammed into a boulder and came to a stop, muscles screaming. Groaning, Emily closed her eyes. Footsteps pounded toward her, and she cracked her eyelids.

Gerard bent over her, concern darkening his eyes and etching lines in his face. Tania's face appeared behind him, her expression a mixture of disgust and frustration. Lips curled, she spat out, "*Faire attention!* Watch where you are going. I told you the journey would be strenuous. We have barely begun, and you—"

"Enough." Gerard held up his hand. "Berating her will not improve the situation."

"This incident has added more risk to an already dangerous trip."

Emily's face heated. She struggled to sit up, and a pain knifed her side. She gasped. "I'm sorry. You're right. I failed to pay attention. Give me a moment, and we can continue."

Gerard shook his head. "You need more than a minute." He shed his pack and settled on the ground next to her. He glanced at Tania then jerked his head toward the top of the hill. She frowned and stomped off. "Does it feel like any bones are broken?"

She shook her head. "No."

"Good. Let me check the extent of your injuries." He ran his fingers through her hair, and she sucked in a breath when he came in contact with the bump pushing through her scalp. "Sorry." His touch light, he continued to check her shoulders, back, and legs before gently moving each foot. "Any pain when I do that? We need to determine if you sprained either ankle."

"I hurt like I've been beaten, but I don't believe I have serious injuries."

"That knot on your skull bears watching." He took her head between his hands and stared into her eyes. His expression softened.

She trembled at his touch.

He removed his hands and dropped them to his lap. "Your pupils aren't sluggish. I don't think you have a concussion."

"I'm sorry for endangering us." She ducked her head and picked at her dirt-encrusted nails.

"Nonsense." He put his finger under her chin and lifted her head until her eyes met his. "Your fall was an accident and could have happened to any of us, even the intrepid Tania."

Emily lost herself in his gaze. What would it be like for him to care about her for real? She blinked and licked her lips. "I appreciate you saying that. I'll do my best to believe your words."

Gerard opened his pack and pulled out his canteen. He unscrewed the lid and held it to her mouth. Tepid water trickled down her throat. He pulled it away, and she nodded.

She brushed the debris from her clothes. "I'm ready. Or as ready as I'll ever be."

Wrapping his left arm around her shoulder, Gerard gripped her fingers with his right hand and helped her to her feet. Her muscles protested, the bruises already making themselves evident with shooting pains. He continued to hold her while she gained her balance, the warmth of his closeness permeating her clothes. She tried not to notice how perfectly she fit against his side, her head tucked beneath his chin. His musky scent filled her nose, and she closed her eyes.

"Something wrong?" His voice resonated with worry.

Her eyes flew open, and she shook her head. She moved out of his grasp, her body immediately bereft of his warmth. "No…well, other than the sensation I was run over by a truck." She cocked her head and forced a smile. "Just another day in France."

He chuckled and stroked her arm. "You're a good sport. I'm sure you can make your way up the hill, but grab my arm for support. Okay?"

She giggled then stopped when the movement sent knives of pain to her middle. "You're learning. I hurt badly enough. I'm glad to accept your help."

His eyebrows shot up, and he mugged an exaggerated look of shock. "You must being in bad shape."

"Funny." She slapped his arm, her heart dancing at his teasing. With her hand tucked in the crook of his arm, they ascended the bluff toward Tania who stood at the top, arms crossed, her face a mask.

Moments later they arrived by her side, and without a word, continued their hike through the woods. Emily lost track of time as she put one sore foot in front of the other. The sun dipped below the trees, dimming the light around them. Gerard periodically grabbed her hand to guide her over an uneven patch of terrain.

Hours passed. Night began to fall. Emily stumbled, and Gerard caught her, his arms firm around her waist. She leaned against him, and tears filled her eyes. She blinked them away. "Thank you. I'm not sure how much longer I can walk. You and Tania should leave me behind and finish the journey. I'll make my way the best I can."

"No. We're in this together. I'll always be a military man despite my shortcomings during that chapter of my life, and we never leave our people behind." He snapped his fingers at their guide.

She turned. "*Que?*"

"We need to stop for a bit. Emily should rest."

Tania frowned, and Emily shook her head. "No. I can walk."

"It is only half a kilometer more. We have taken too long already. You must push yourself."

Gerard leaned down and peered into Emily's face. "I can carry you."

"Hauling me and both packs is too much and will slow us down even further. Now that I know we're almost at the end of the journey…well, at least this leg…I can make it." She pasted a grin on her face. "But don't expect me to cook dinner or clean house when we arrive."

He snickered and pulled her into an embrace. "Promise."

Emily sagged against his firm chest. Did he never tire? When was the last time she'd been this exhausted? Never, if truth be told. Any complaints about fatigue faded in light of the endless tramping over miles of woodland. She breathed deeply of his scent, a musky mixture of leather and perspiration, then straightened her spine and moved away from the comfort of his arms. She pushed her bedraggled hair away from her face. "All right. Let's move out. We've got a way station to find, and it won't be light for much longer."

He tucked a stray strand of hair behind her ear then ran his finger down her jawline.

She shivered, and her eyes widened. His expression was unreadable in the growing dusk. She grasped the straps of her pack and marched forward avoiding Tania's scrutiny.

They hiked for about fifteen minutes and came to a clearing. The dark shape of a building huddled at the other end of the expanse. Relief was in sight. Emily stepped forward.

Tania grabbed her arm. "Wait. Something is amiss."

"I don't sense anything."

Beside her, Gerard tensed. The hair on the back of her neck prickled. Her heart pounded, and her eyes strained to see. Listening to the night sounds, she cocked her head. There…mingled amid the crickets and rustling of animals, who prowled at night…the murmur of voices. A chill swept over her. Outlined against the trees, shadowy figures exited the tiny cottage. The wind carried their words toward her.

"Nein. Nothing…the spies…come here."

Emily whipped her head toward Gerard and Tania, whose fear and surprise were evident even in the blackness.

The Germans continued to talk. "Should…wait?"

"We've…a full day. You remain…we'll seek the American girl and…bald partner elsewhere."

"I thought…her husband."

"Nein. Sources say their marriage…a sham. Part of…disguise. We'll get them….can't…far." The figure turned, and his voice ceased to carry.

A moment later, his underling saluted. "Jawohl."

Emily wrapped her arms around her middle, perspiration forming at her hairline. Her heart threatened to jump from her chest. If not for

Tania's senses being on high alert, they would have been caught. Breathing jagged, she fought to quell the rising panic.

An engine roared to life. Seconds later, a sedan rumbled from behind the house and drove away, taillights fading as it bumped its way down the narrow road.

Tania crossed her arms. "The location has obviously been compromised." Her voice was barely above a whisper. "I must report the situation, but there's no time. We must push on." She jerked her head toward the building. "He may decide to patrol. There is another safe house a few kilometers from here."

Emily's shoulders slumped. Dear Lord, give me strength to continue. I don't think I can walk another step, but our safety depends on me.

"How many is a few?" Gerard asked.

"Four."

He nodded. "Okay, but we wait until he's moved to the other side of the house before we proceed. I don't want to risk him hearing us, even as far away as he is." A moment later, the soldier's figure disappeared around the edge of the cottage. "Good, he is gone." He slipped one arm out of the straps of his backpack. "Give me your satchel. I will carry it."

She hesitated then nodded and allowed him to remove the bag from her back, the weight sliding from body. A breeze ruffled her shirt, cooling the perspiration trickling down her spine.

Gerard slung her pack over his other shoulder. "Better?"

"If possible, it has gotten heavier the longer we've trekked."

He chucked her under the chin. "You must be tired."

Tania leaned toward them. "It is not my decision. I am just an operative, but I suggest you change your plans and find a church where you can get married for real. You heard those men. They know your identities and your cover story. You must change the details, and one way is to add truth to the lies. I know a priest."

## Chapter Sixteen

Gerard shoved aside the blackout curtains inside the closet-sized room. Murky sunlight seeped through the grimy windowpanes. His eyes burned, but between the adrenaline rush from the near miss with the Germans and the additional kilometers of slogging through the woods, sleep had eluded him. He rotated his shoulders, but the muscles remained knotted.

Was Emily awake yet? Had she managed to get any shut-eye? By the time they stumbled through the door to the safe house, her face was ashen with fatigue, her eyes red rimmed and bloodshot. She swayed on her feet as he led her to an identical miniscule room next to his. A ragdoll had more substance. He'd removed her shoes and covered her with a threadbare blanket, but her eyes remained open, watching his every move as if she couldn't bring herself to close them.

Tania left without entering after assuring them another operative would arrive at dusk for the next leg of their journey. She'd pressed a paper into his hand that contained the name and address of the church where the priest was friendly to the cause, as she'd put it.

Emily had not replied to Tania's suggestion for them to marry in actuality, and the emotions that danced across her face were a mixture of wonder, confusion, and something unreadable. She'd been upset when she found out about the ruse as part of their assignment. How did she feel about the proposition to make their relationship real? Over the days they'd been in France, their friendship seemed to have deepened. She was no longer as defensive and had responded to his teasing on several occasions, even going so far as to taunt him in return.

In the past, the thought of entering into matrimony had gripped him with myriad emotions, fear the least of them. Yet no anxiety plagued him when he unfurled the scrap and studied Tania's scrawl.

He bowed his head. "Dear God, we haven't been on speaking terms, and I'm beginning to see how wrong I was to walk away from You because of my anger at my brother's death. I'm sorry about that, and I hope You'll forgive me. I don't want to hurt Emily or ruin her reputation back in England, but is this plan from You? You've kept us safe thus far without our interference, but I've read enough of the Bible to know that sometimes You use unconventional methods to save Your people. Let Emily know what You'd have us do…um, I guess that's it. Thanks for listening…Amen."

Warmth enveloped him, and Gerard's eyes moistened. He didn't deserve God's mercy, but apparently He saw fit to grant it. There was no other explanation for the feeling of peace that seemed to fill him from head to foot. His army buddies would think he'd gone soft or even lost his mind. So be it. Over the course of the mission, there'd been too many times they should have been caught and weren't. Not coincidence. Of that he was sure.

A faint knock sounded, and he blinked. Running his hand over the stubble that had begun to cover his scalp, he opened the door. Emily stood on the threshold, her lower lip caught between her teeth. Her face shone from scrubbing, and her hair was brushed and gleaming. She tilted her head. "Are you okay? You look…different."

"I am. How are you feeling after your fall?"

"Sore, but the pain is manageable."

He nodded. "That's good news. I don't know about you, but I'm famished. Did they leave us anything to eat?"

"There are some potatoes, turnips, parsnips, and eggs. Oh, and a tiny lump of cheese. The vegetables look a little tired, but they're probably from someone's root cellar, and we're blessed to have them."

He rubbed his hands together. "Then how about my famous cheese omelet with a side of home fries."

She giggled. "Famous? Right, because no one has ever heard of putting cheese in an omelet."

"Maybe." He gestured toward the kitchen. "Lead on, MacDuff."

"Culinary skills and a Shakespearean actor?" She pressed a hand to her heart in mock wonder. "Such hidden talents, Major Lucas."

With a chuckle, he opened the drawers until he found a knife, spatula, and two skillets. "You have no idea. Now, how about you peel the vegetables and chop them into small cubes. I'll handle the eggs."

"Because it's such a specialized dish."

"Exactly."

He lit the stove under the pans to heat them then stood next to her at the counter where they prepped the meal. He glanced at her and swallowed a smile. Her lips were pressed together, and a tiny wrinkle appeared between her eyebrows as she tried to pare the skin from the vegetables with a knife that probably hadn't been sharpened since long before Hitler's arrival. As before, he stifled the desire to smooth her forehead. He blew out a breath and cracked the eggs into a chipped porcelain bowl, then whipped them into a froth with a bent fork.

She cleared her throat. "Are you going to tell me what happened to you between last night and this morning? Despite our immediate danger and the outlandish suggestion by Tania for us to wed, you seem as relaxed as if we were on holiday."

He shrugged. "You remember the story in the Bible where Jacob wrestled with God? I couldn't sleep, so God used the opportunity to reach out to me. We had an...er...extensive conversation. I confessed my anger and a bunch of other stuff, and asked Him to forgive me. I'm sure I'll still mess up, but I gave Him control of the situation."

"Gerard, that's wonderful." She laid down the knife and wrapped him in a hug, a clean, soapy scent wafting from her hair. He closed his eyes and returned her embrace. Her heart beat against his chest, causing his own to speed up. Lord, help me. I'm beginning to care for this woman.

His stomach rumbled, and his faced warmed. So much for their intimate moment.

Emily pulled away and ducked her head, a smile tugging at the corner of her mouth. "You *are* hungry." She sobered up. "Eat your fill. Who knows when we'll get our next meal?"

"About that…uh…have you given further consideration to Tania's recommendation?" He pulled the sheet from his pocket and laid it on the counter, the black letters and numbers stark against the paper.

She nibbled her lower lip, his favorite habit of hers, then her head moved in an imperceptible nod.

"And?"

"I think we should take her recommendation." Her voice was barely above a whisper, and her cheeks were tinged pink.

"I agree. We can have it annulled upon our return to England, and no one will be the wiser. You sure you're okay with this?"

"Yes. Tania is with the local Resistance. She knows the best way to evade the authorities. If she says a real marriage certificate is the most advantageous way for us to escape notice, then I'm all for it."

"Okay, do you need time to get ready, or should we go after breakfast."

Emily gestured to her clothes, a bulky sweater over faded blue slacks and scuffed oxfords. "I didn't happen to bring my trousseau, so any time is fine with me."

"Not exactly what you planned to wear for your wedding, is it?"

"No, but then I didn't think I'd be getting married in France while running for my life."

"Well, there is that." He swallowed without telling her she looked beautiful no matter what she wore, then turned to the stove and made quick work of cooking their food, the fragrant aroma causing his stomach to speak up again.

"Better hurry." She giggled. "Apparently, you're close to fainting." She laid silverware on the scarred wooden table then rummaged in the cabinet for glasses that she filled from the spigot. Seating herself in one of the rickety chairs, she folded her hands in her lap.

Gerard dished the food onto chipped plates and brought them to the table. Lowering himself into the chair next to her, he held out his hand. "I'm new at this, but I thought I'd ask the blessing for our meal."

Her face lit up, and she grasped his fingers, her hand small and warm. "I'd like that."

He bowed his head for the second time that morning. "Uh, dear God, please bless this food to keep us strong for the journey. Thank You for those who left it in the house, and for the work they are doing to fight the evil threatening this land. Please keep us safe as we travel, and…um…if we're not supposed to get married, please let us know. Uh…thanks for all You're doing. Amen."

Emily squeezed his hand then forked a bit of egg into her mouth. She moaned and closed her eyes. "This should be famous."

"Yeah, your hunger has nothing to do with how good it tastes."

The room filled with her laughter, and he grinned. He looked forward to making her laugh more often.

They ate quickly and were soon ready to leave. He closed the door behind them, and they hurried down the dirt path that led into the village. The church spire soared above the tiny town, making it easy to find the stone structure at the end of the square. He gestured to the open door. "Another sign we're on the right track?"

"I'm going to say yes."

He led her inside, the air cooling as they entered the foyer. Moving through the door into the sanctuary, he surveyed the beautiful room. Stained glass windows cast rainbows of color across the pews. An altar stood at the front flanked by a pair of six-foot-tall candlesticks. Several ornate chairs graced the dais. A stooped, balding man in robes looked up from behind a table filled with candles. He strode in their direction. "Friends of Tania?"

Gerard's eyes widened. "How did you—"

"She said you might come by. We've been waiting for you."

"We?" He shook his head. The man must think him an imbecile.

"I'm Father Victor." He clapped his hands, and a side door opened. An elderly man in a suit and two women slipped into the room. "Doreen and Celeste will be your witnesses. This is Adam Reneau. He is the mayor of our fine town."

Gerard's hand flew to the pistol tucked in the waistband of his pants.

Father Victor held up his hands. "Wait. Listen to me. In order for the marriage to be official it must be performed by the mayor. Any ceremony I conduct will only be symbolic."

"Then why did Tania have us come here? To involve you?"

"Because it made more sense for me to coordinate the event. She probably knew you wouldn't believe her when she told you the mayor is not Vichy."

Gerard narrowed his eyes. "Why should we believe you?"

"You can choose not to, but Adam is my brother, and we provide a variety of services for loyal French and others who need it. He is able to, shall we say, expedite your papers. He will give you everything you need to travel."

Emily laid her hand on Gerard's arm. "If he were here to arrest us, he would not have waited for an introduction. God has provided the means for us to marry in the eyes of the law and of the church. Let's be grateful."

He huffed out a breath, and he released his hold on his weapon. His newfound faith had crumbled at the first glimmer of difficulty. He dipped his head toward the men. "My apologies for assuming the worst."

Father Victor looked at Emily. "Mademoiselle, please follow these ladies. They will help you get ready."

The women led Emily to the door, and with a look over her shoulder she disappeared.

Father Victor laid his hand on Gerard's arm. "Tania indicated this…uh…arrangement is to keep you safe from the authorities. I was going to counsel you on the seriousness of your decision to wed for such a reason, but it appears by your expression that this is no cavalier agreement. Does she know how you feel about her?"

"No." He looked deep into the priest's eyes. "And I don't want to hurt her. I will treat her as she deserves."

"Very well."

An eternity seemed to pass before the door opened, and Emily appeared dressed in an ivory suit, with a matching pillbox hat. A small veil attached to the hat covered her eyes, and she gripped a bouquet of wildflowers. Her face glowed.

His breath caught. What had he gotten himself into?

Chapter Seventeen

Emily's heart beat like a timpani in Bach's *Christmas Oratorio*. Across the sanctuary, Gerard stood next to the priest whose serene expression belied the seriousness of their situation. She tugged at the skirt of her borrowed suit and nibbled her lower lip. The ladies treated her like a normal bride-to-be, giggling and smiling as they helped her prepare for her nuptials.

Convinced she would arrive, the woman had everything ready for her, including a blue ribbon tied around the flower stems. Apparently, somewhere along the way, they'd learned about the English tradition. With lightning speed, they produced her outfit and swept her hair into an elegant chignon, then pinned the small hat on top. The bouquet, clutched between her damp palms, was a collection of pink, yellow, and purple blooms, most of which she didn't recognize.

Doreen gestured toward Emily's prospective groom. "You are beautiful, and from the look on his face, your young man seems to agree. Let's get you married." She nudged her from behind.

"Yes, of course." Emily gripped the flowers tighter and walked toward the men, Doreen and Celeste following close on her heels. Emily took a deep breath. *Dear Lord, please give me a sign that this is right. Marriage is sacred, and I don't want to go against Your will.*

She arrived at Gerard's side and looked up at him through her veil. His gaze probed her own, seeming to question whether she was ready, but at the same time indicating he would do what she wished. The tightness in her chest eased. She would take his attitude as her sign from God. She passed her bouquet to Doreen and smiled.

Gerard winked and reached for her hand. His warm, calloused fingers enveloped hers, sending tingles up her arm. She nibbled her lower lip, and his eyes moved to her mouth as he squeezed her fingers. Her face heated.

Mayor Reneau cleared his throat. "*Commençons.* Let's begin." He turned to Gerard. "Repeat after me. *Moi, Gerard, je te prend Emily...*"

Gerard's rumbling voice echoed the vows as prompted. Emily swallowed. She was getting married. How would her family respond if they knew?

Soon it was time to say her vows, and minutes later the civil ceremony was complete. The priest stepped forward and opened his Bible. "You are married in the eyes of the law, but I wish to say a few words to take with you on your journey as husband and wife." Tissue papers rustled as he turned the pages. "Yes, here we are. In Ecclesiastes Chapter Four we read that a threefold cord is not quickly broken. You are both followers of Jesus, oui?" He peered at Emily and Gerard.

"Yes," they murmured in unison.

"Bon. You are a threefold cord." A smile creased his face. "I cannot promise that life together will be easy, especially now in a time of war, but when you lean on God during the good and the bad, you will have a strength that passes human understanding. You will have peace where others have strife. You will have wisdom where others have foolishness. Walk side by side, no matter what, and your cord will not be broken." He closed his Bible. "You may kiss your bride."

Emily's palms moistened, and her heart stuttered. How could she have forgotten about this part of the ceremony?

Gerard pulled up her veil and dipped his head then stopped a fraction of an inch above her lips for a second before pressing his mouth on hers. His lips were firm yet gentle, and then they were gone, leaving her bereft. Warmth spread from her stomach to her limbs, and her toes curled. He tucked a loose strand of hair behind her ear, and she leaned into his touch. His crystal-blue eyes widened.

Her face heated, and she straightened. What must he think of her, acting as if their marriage was real? Whether she intended to or not, she had fallen in love with this headstrong, infuriating, charming, intelligent, and very good-looking man. Her heart constricted. She could never let him know. Even though his behavior had changed, and he was gracious and nice to her, it was improbable he felt more than friendship.

Mayor Reneau cleared his throat. "We must complete the paperwork." He pulled out a sheet of paper from his breast pocket and indicated where they were to sign. Reaching into his pocket again, he withdrew two French passports. "These are your new identities. Congratulations, Monsieur and Madame Paquet. I wish you the best in your marriage." He dipped his head in a curt nod, lifted his hand in farewell, and strode to the back of the church where he headed out the door.

Emily stared at the passport then looked at Gerard. "Will I ever get used to how quickly things change?"

"You may not believe me, but you will."

Celeste pointed to a small table that held two lumps of cheese and a fruit tart. "It is not a wedding cake, but the best we could do on short notice."

Emily turned. "How special. We appreciate everything you've done for us." She jabbed Gerard who seemed enamored with the cheese.

"Uh...oui...it is a day I will not forget."

"We hope not. It's your wedding day."

He blanched, then his face reddened to his hairline.

Emily studied him. Nice to see Gerard discomfited for once. Was he embarrassed, or did he regret his decision to go through with the marriage? She picked up the knife, cut a piece of the tart, and held it to his mouth. "As she said, it's not wedding cake, but it will do in a pinch."

Gerard smiled, and his eyes crinkled at the edges. He cut a chunk from the pastry and picked it up. "How does it go? Down the hatch? Open wide and down the slide?"

She laughed, and he tucked the bite into her mouth then grabbed her arm and guided her hand to feed him. His lips closed around her fingers, and she drew in a breath. She jumped as if burned, yanking her hand away.

He chuckled and reached to cut more tart. "I can get used to this."

"Well, don't. I happen to know you're quite capable of feeding yourself." Her heart continued to pound in response to his playfulness.

Doreen reached under the tablecloth and pulled out a pair of champagne glasses and a bottle of wine. A self-satisfied smile lit up her face. "We were also able to secure some wine. Unfortunately, the German occupiers have availed themselves of the best France has to offer, but we hope you find this acceptable. It is from a local vineyard, sent with their compliments."

"And we are grateful."

Gerard popped the cork and poured the straw-colored liquid. He cocked his head. "Surely, you plan to join us."

"We only have two glasses."

"Then we'll share." Emily started to sip from the glass.

"Wait." With a saucy grin, Gerard linked his arm through hers. "Now, we toast."

The fizzy drink slid down Emily's throat. "Granted, my experience with wine is limited, but this is delicious. It tastes like apples, too." She extricated herself and handed her glass to Doreen.

Father Victor rubbed his hands together. "A beautiful ceremony despite the circumstances, and I'm sorry to cut off the festivities, but we must get you on the road. You need to reach your destination before curfew."

A chill swept over Emily, and she pressed a hand over her stomach where the drums had started beating again. In the blink of an eye, the harsh reality of her life was back.

Chapter Eighteen

The sanctuary door opened with a bang.

Gerard's head whipped around. A pair of German SS officers tromped up the aisle toward the celebrants. Next to him, Emily's body had stiffened, and she clutched his arm in a viselike grip. Celeste and Doreen stood at the food table, hands frozen in the act of slicing the tart. Pinning an obsequious smile and what he hoped was a look of innocence on his face, Gerard dipped his head toward the soldiers.

Behind the altar, Father Victor pressed his palms together. "Welcome back, *Standartenführer* Weber and *Hauptsturmführer* Schneider. It is an honor to see you again."

Weber, the taller of the two officers clicked together the heels of his gleaming knee-high boots. The leather of his gun belt squeaked as he bowed. His white-blond hair contrasted with his heavily tanned face. Piercing blue eyes were set deep in his face. One eyebrow was separated by a deep comma-shaped scar. "I heard there was yet another wedding and wanted to congratulate the newlyweds." He peered at Gerard and Emily. "Is this the happy couple?"

Gerard nodded and wrapped his arm around Emily's shoulder.

Father Victor smiled. "Oui. You are just in time to see them off. This is Sophie and Jules Boucher. Jules works at the *la manufacture*."

"Ah, doing your part for *der führer*. Excellent. I wondered why such a young man was not in uniform or"—he sneered—"hiding underground." Weber stepped toward to Emily. "And do you work as well, Frau Boucher?"

"I am *la professeure*. I teach the small children." Her voice trembled, and Gerard drew her closer, her frame rigid in his arms.

He bounced on his toes. "My wife, she is too modest. Oui, she is a teacher but so much more than that. The children love her as they would a mother."

"I can understand why." He leered at Emily and ran a gloved finger along her jaw. "And she is beautiful. You certainly got the full package with your young wife."

Gerard's hand fisted, and he shoved it in his pocket to prevent him from punching the wolfish expression on the man's face. Was the officer trying to get a rise out of him, or was he simply a lecher? "Oui." He would play along. "And I am grateful she would marry such a man as me. I don't deserve her love."

Seeming to overcome her trepidation, Emily fluttered her eyelashes. "Now it is my *mari* who is modest. He is strong as an ox and has already provided for me. And he is doing his part for the cause." She raised her arm. "Heil, Hitler."

Gerard squeezed her arm. Atta girl, Emily. What else could they say or do to get these goons out of the church? If he did anything to indicate he and Emily were in a hurry to leave, the soldiers might get suspicious.

The officers held up their hands. "Heil, Hitler." Their voices bounced off the stone walls and wooden floor.

Father Victor gestured to Weber and Schneider. "Won't you join us for some refreshments? They are humble offerings, but we hope you find them to your liking."

"Nein. We must be on our way." Weber looked down his nose. "Too bad you didn't make a *Baumkuchen*. A German wedding cake would ensure a long, happy marriage. At least, that's what my *Großmutter* used to say. I wouldn't know."

Schneider nudged his commanding officer and handed him a small package. "The gift, sir."

"Ah, yes. We have brought a small token of respect for this blessed occasion." He rocked back on his heels and puffed out his chest. "To celebrate the love of this lovely young couple who are supporters of the Reich and couldn't possibly be tied to any nefarious schemes." Sarcasm dripped from his words as he tapped his chin with his index finger. "Two uncomplicated people who have found affection in a time of war."

Gerard's chest tightened. Would the soldiers never leave? Was their graciousness a show, and the colonel came to arrest them both or was he just an arrogant puppet in Hitler's ranks who enjoyed lording his power over the populace?

With a pompous smile, Weber held out the gift, a photograph of Hitler encased in a silver frame. "Now, you can start your marriage right. Every good and loyal home should have a picture of der führer watching over it."

"Merci." Emily reached for the portrait then curtsied. "You do us a great honor with your presence and with your gift. We thank you."

"You're welcome." His eyes gleamed. "I don't suppose you are wealthy enough to afford a honeymoon. Too bad you can't visit some of Germany's beautiful sites such as Neuschwanstein Castle or the Cologne Cathedral. You will have to settle for France." He sneered.

Gerard shook his head. "No, we have little money for that, but even so, travel papers are difficult to obtain, sir. We will spend a quiet day at home, then I must return to work."

"Bah! Stupid government minions. I will take care of this." He rifled through his pockets then glanced at Schneider. "Do you have any paper with you?"

Schneider pulled a folded sheet from his inside breast pocket. "Only this, sir, but it is the order we…uh…received this morning."

"Perfect." Weber snatched the missive and tore it, separating the typewritten words and the masthead of the German High Command. He laid the paper on the altar and retrieved a fountain pen from his pocket.

Unscrewing the lid, he scribbled below the emblem, the nib scratching across the ivory stationery.

Gerard widened his eyes. Was the colonel actually writing them travel orders? Would this give them free passage across France? Perhaps, God was moving in one of His mysterious ways and using a pawn of the Nazis to grant Emily and him freedom.

Weber picked up the paper and blew on it, drying the ink. He handed it to Gerard. "I have important business to attend to, or I would escort you myself. Take this to my office, and ask for Müller. Explain the situation, and he will issue your travel papers. Retain this, and should you have any problems, you may use my name which should iron out any possible wrinkle you encounter." He preened, reminiscent of the peacock Gerard had seen at the San Diego Zoo years ago when life was serene and war was unheard of, then reached into his pocket and pulled out several *reichsmarks* that he pressed into Gerard's hand.

"Merci...*uh*...*Dankeschön*." Gerard bowed. "You have been most kind to us. We are lowly French peasants, yet you have graced us with your company and bestowed these wonderful gifts. We will never forget what you have done."

"As you shouldn't." Weber looked down his nose then snapped his fingers. "Schneider, let us depart. We have much to do." He nudged Gerard's shoulder and winked. "Enjoy your honeymoon." He pivoted and marched down the aisle, his aide close behind him. They left the church, and the door closed with a thud.

Father Victor blew out a loud breath. "I was afraid he would partake of the wine and discover that the Germans are not receiving all of our best vintages."

Emily sagged against him, and Gerard supported her diminutive figure with his arm, breathing in the scent of her skin and hair. "That was a close one, indeed." He held up the picture and frowned. "And who did he *transport* to obtain this valuable frame?"

"Despicable as the gift is, you must carry it in your luggage in case you are searched." Father Victor sighed. "It will be another layer of duplicity to make it seem you are a loyal German subject."

"Good point. We should be grateful that he wasn't here to take us away." Gerard glanced at the food and swallowed. "I've lost my appetite. Please share our largesse with one of your poorer families." He peered down at Emily's wan face, and his heart skittered. "We should go to his office immediately and secure the visas before he comes to his senses that giving a young French couple authority to travel unrestricted through the country is a bad idea."

She nodded and straightened her spine, pulling away. She brushed errant strands of hair away from her face. "Give me a few minutes to change my clothes."

He laid his hand on her arm then leaned forward and kissed her forehead. "You were a beautiful bride."

Her face flushed, and she ducked her head. "Thank you." She scuttled toward the side door.

The women busied themselves with packing up the food and drink. Moments later, they too left the sanctuary through the side door.

"You must tell her how you feel, monsieur." Father Victor crossed his arms.

"No. Emotions cloud judgment, and that is unacceptable on a mission." Gerard shook his head. "Besides, she couldn't possible feel anything for me, so it would only hurt her to make any sort of declaration."

Emily appeared in the doorway, dressed in dark slacks and a white blouse, satchel in one hand and a jacket slung over the other arm.

He pressed his lips together. Had she heard their conversation? He studied her expression which only held fatigue and anticipation. "Ready?"

"As I'll ever be." She wrinkled her nose. "Do missions ever go as expected?"

With a chuckle, he reached for her bag. "Oftentimes, yes, but now you know why we trained for the unexpected."

She turned to the priest. "Thank you, Father. I will pray for your safety and that of your flock. God bless you and your work."

Father Victor made the sign of the cross. "And you, my daughter."

Gerard bent his arm, and she slipped her hand in the crook of his elbow. The pressure of her fingers through his shirt warmed him. His grip tightened on her valise, and they hurried from the church. "Can you believe our luck?"

"Luck had nothing to do with it. His decision to give us travel papers was a miracle, and that man has no idea he was an instrument of God." She giggled. "Bet that wouldn't go down too well with him."

"Not in the least." He scanned their surroundings as they made their way to the German's office. Women swept their front steps, and children played stickball in the street. In the distance, a dog barked. Two elderly men sat on a bench reading newspapers. The idyllic scenes belied the war's intrigue and conflict. Were these people who they seemed— simple villagers who only wanted to provide for their families?

One of the old men met his gaze before turning back to his companion. Or was the Resistance as strong as Father Victor eluded to? Who among these people was part of the underground society bent on overthrowing their occupiers?

His neck stiffened. Were there sympathizers in their midst who would rat out a neighbor for a crust of bread or a few coins?

"Are you okay?" Emily's brow was wrinkled. "Foolish question considering the fact we're on our way to the German command office, but you seem extra alert."

"I can't shake the feeling of impending doom...well, not doom exactly, but tension. It seems to hang over the entire village. Makes me wonder what I'm not seeing. I also wonder if we're being set up, and the offer of a visa is a ruse to get us to office where we can be arrested with ease."

She shook her head. "That doesn't strike me as the Germans' style. The news stories I read report very public arrests, as if the occupiers are proving their right to apprehend certain people. Subtlety doesn't seem to be their way of operating."

They arrived at the squat building that housed Standartenführer Weber and his staff. Gerard took a deep breath, but heaviness continued to weigh on him. He forced a smile. "Let's get this over with."

Emily patted her hair and nodded.

Gerard opened the door, and they entered the ornate foyer. A large portrait of Hitler hung on the wall above a uniformed soldier seated at a wooden desk, his fingers pecking at the cumbersome typewriter in front of him. The Nazi flag was draped on the railing on the second floor. Sunlight shone on the polished tile floor.

The soldier raised his head and squinted at them. "What are you doing here? Your presence is highly irregular. This is a military facility."

Before Gerard could respond, Emily scurried forward, her hand pressed to her chest. "We just got married, and you won't believe what happened. We can hardly believe it ourselves. After the ceremony, Standartenführer Weber arrived to bestow his congratulations. We are so honored he would deign to come to the church. That in itself is amazing, but then he gave us this lovely gift." She held out the picture. "Now we can start our marriage out right. We're so happy—"

"Enough!" The young man scowled. "None of that tells me why you have the audacity to enter."

She flinched, then laid the signed paper on the desk. "My apologies. I'm just so excited about our good fortune thanks to your Standartenführer. He gave us this authorization and told us to come here to secure our visa. You see, we didn't have the necessary travel papers to take a proper honeymoon, and when he found out, he wrote us this letter." She fluttered her eyelashes, her voice breathless. "Isn't that incredible. Such a generous man. We are so blessed. Wouldn't you agree?"

Gerard swallowed a smile. Emily was laying it on thick, but the soldier seemed to be buying the whole performance. Oscar winner Joan Fontaine couldn't hold a candle to his partner.

"Highly irregular." He grabbed the paper and held it close for several minutes. Finally, when Gerard was sure he'd claim it was a forgery, he tossed it down then yanked open the center drawer. He rummaged among the folders and forms, his lips moving in silent complaint. He withdrew a travel pass and held out his hand. "Your identity cards."

Gerard pulled them from his breast pocket.

The man flipped open the books, transferred the information onto the form, and flung everything back at Gerard. "Now, you need to leave."

Emily curtsied and continued to bat her eyes. Wreathed in smiles, her face beamed. "Thank you, sir. You've been most helpful. God bless you."

They whirled and hurried from the building, Gerard's breath ragged, waiting for the man's shout to halt. Could their escape from France be this easy?

Once outside, Emily skipped head of him then turned and beckoned him forward. Rolling her eyes, she wrinkled her nose. "Highly irregular," she mimicked. "I thought we were goners for a few seconds, didn't you?"

"Not with your Academy Award-winning performance."

She laughed. "They call themselves the master race, yet he was so gullible. He actually believed we're in love. Stupid fellow."

Gerard's heart fell. He'd begun to think she might have feelings for him. Now, who was stupid?

## Chapter Nineteen

Emily shifted on the buffed leather seat in the train compartment to break the mesmerizing clickety-clack of the wheels that threatened her ability to stay awake. If she napped now, she'd never sleep tonight. Beside her, Gerard sat with his arms crossed, eyes closed, and gray fedora pulled low over his face. Anyone who didn't know him would think he dozed. His rigid frame told her differently. She wasn't sure he ever slept more than a couple of hours a night. How he managed to remain vigilant was a mystery.

She frowned. After their success with the travel visa, he'd become surly and morose. When questioned, he insisted nothing was wrong. Yet, he'd been as irascible as a wounded mountain lion, giving one word answers and glowering at everyone they'd been in contact with from the porter to fellow travelers.

The scenery outside the window whizzed past in a blur. Countryside greens and blues changed to grays and browns when they passed through towns. She glanced at her watch. Still several hours until bedtime when she and Gerard would make their way to the sleeper car he insisted they purchase to further their guise as a newly married couple. Her face heated. It would be a long night.

Hurtling across the French countryside in fear for her life was not what she'd planned for her honeymoon. She rolled her eyes. Who was she kidding? She never figured on getting married, so planning a trip with a husband was not on her to-do list, yet here she was tied to Gerard *for better or for worse.* Could it get any worse?

Another peek at her watch, and she sighed. Three minutes had passed since she last checked.

A gentle knock sounded at the door, and the porter waved through the window. He slid open the wooden divider, and an elderly couple appeared behind him. "Monsieur and Madame Boucher, may I present Monsieur and Madame Vidal? They will be sharing your compartment for a short while. I apologize for any inconvenience."

Emily scooted close to Gerard who sat up and shoved his hat back on his head. His body stiffened, but he remained mute.

She nodded at the couple. Why did they need to share the compartment? Was it a ploy to get close to Gerard and her? Where did their loyalties lie?

"Merci. We appreciate your gracious hospitality." Madame Vidal gripped her husband's arm as she toddled into the small alcove. Her diminutive hat was a confection of flowers and netting that wiggled with each movement of her head. Although expensive-looking, her navy-blue suit had seen better days, and her black pumps were scuffed. "The attendant said you just got married. *Félicitations.* How optimistic of you in a time of war."

Snuggling into Gerard, Emily grinned. "We are so happy. Aren't we, *chéri*?" She stroked his arm and affected a high-pitched giggle.

Gerard cleared his throat. "Oui. We were tired of waiting for the end of the war. It seems the conflict will never cease."

The woman peered down her nose. "You are not in uniform. Do you not fight for the cause?"

He shook his head. "I work in the factory. We were able to secure a travel visa for this short trip. I must return in two days." He ran a finger along the side of Emily's face, and she shivered. "Not nearly enough time to spend with my bride."

Monsieur Vidal chuckled. "There is never enough time. We have been married for nearly fifty years, and yet it feels like yesterday that I met this beautiful, feisty woman."

"Fifty years? You must have been children when you married." Gerard extended his hand, and the man shook it.

"How gallant of you to say, young man." Madame Vidal patted her hair causing the hat to slip to one side.

Emily's face ached from smiling. How long before the couple departed? "We're heading to Paris to see the sights. Are you?"

Madame Vidal waved her hand in dismissal. "Non. We are too old for the crowds and chaos. And all those…Germans." She grimaced. "The next stop is ours. Our daughter lives outside the city." Her face fell. "We used to take in the sights. The Eiffel Tower. The Arc de Triomphe. The Louvre. Those were the days, weren't they, *amoureux*?"

Her husband laced his fingers with hers. "And they will be again, someday. Now, let us speak of happier things, such as this lovely couple. How did you meet?"

Emily swallowed. As her favorite detective would say, "The game is afoot."

----·----

Gerard uncrossed his arms and wrapped one around Emily, marveling again at how perfectly she fit against his side. They needed to appear deeply in love, so he would act the part even if a piece of his heart died in the process.

He studied the octogenarians. Were they too old to be of use to the Resistance? Or worse, the Nazis? They seemed harmless enough, but if he'd learned one thing while in combat, it was to never underestimate his opponent. He'd nearly been killed during his first shift on sentry duty in North Africa. A boy of perhaps twelve or thirteen had wandered into camp. Gaunt and dirty like most of the street urchins he'd seen, the lad asked for food and drink. When Gerard had bent to retrieve his ration pack, the waif had pulled a knife. Fortunately, the blade only sliced Gerard's coat and had not pierced his skin, but the boy's wiry frame and tenacity made him difficult to subdue. Gerard's platoon mates ribbed him for days about his inability to overpower a child. He wouldn't make that mistake again.

Emily's shoulder quivered under his hand. His gaze slid from the couple to his wife. Would he ever get used to the term? Her hands were clenched in her lap, yet a smile played on her lips. Apparently, she was as unsure about the elderly pair as he was. He laid his hand over her fists, their warmth sending tingles through his palm.

Her lips trembled. "We met during our last year in *lycée*. I lost my parents in an automobile accident and moved in with my grandparents. It was difficult to be the new girl in school, and Jules was nice to me. We studied together as friends and attended the same university. By the second year of college, we had fallen in love."

"Such a beautiful story." Madame Vidal sighed and pressed her hand over her heart. "Friendship is an important foundation of a successful marriage."

Monsieur Vidal cocked his head. "Yet, it's been a while since your finished university, isn't it? Why did you wait?"

A chill swept over Gerard. Was the man's question one of innocence, or was he probing their story for inconsistences? "We didn't plan to. When the occupation came, I had just graduated. The morning we were to wed, the Germans came through my neighborhood and rounded up all males over the age of twelve. I was terrified I'd be shipped to Germany, but for some reason my group remained in France."

Emily leaned forward. "I was beside myself with worry. I arrived at the town hall for the marriage, and Jules didn't show up. Then I overheard some of the employees talking about the men who were taken, and I knew what happened. Finally, after three months, the workers were allowed to contact their loved ones. It was another three months before I was able to find housing close to the plant so we could see each other on his day off."

"You poor dears. How awful." Madame Vidal entwined her arm with her husband's.

"The Vichy government has been slow in granting marriage licenses." Gerard rubbed his forehead. "We applied months ago, and the authorization just came through."

"How on earth did you get travel visas?" Monsieur Vidal narrowed his eyes. "Those are equally difficult to obtain."

Gerard shrugged and explained the Standartenführer's attendance at their ceremony. "It was fortuitous that he arrived. Otherwise, it would be back to the factory for me."

"Or providential. Sometimes God works in mysterious ways. Isn't that how the saying goes."

"Oui. My wife said the very same thing when the incident occurred. We're not sure why He chose to bless us in this manner, but we're grateful. But enough of our story. You are traveling to see your daughter. How has your journey been?" Would they give him the information he needed to continue their escape?

"Convoluted and arduous." Monsieur Vidal frowned. "As you can imagine, the SS are everywhere. They board trains indiscriminately and conduct searches of people as well as luggage. Heavy handed, the officers take what they want and allow their underlings to harass and terrorize the populace. Disgraceful."

His wife nodded. "I have been *handled* on more than one occasion, and poor Clement could do nothing. If he intervened, they might have arrested him…or worse. Our occupiers are barbarians and seem to take pleasure in boorish behavior."

"Does this occur at every stop?" Gerard's heart pounded. Should he and Emily jump off the train before the next station?

"Very nearly, especially as we approached the city." He pulled his wife closer. "They are why we are sharing your compartment. The train is full, and there are several SS officers who boarded at the last stop and need somewhere to sit. The officer in charge unceremoniously threw us out of our berth. He looked sophisticated enough with his tall stature, blond hair, and clean-cut appearance, but no manners at all, uncivilized really."

Gerard's grip on Emily's hands tightened. Had their pursuer caught up with them?

## Chapter Twenty

The porter appeared at the window then knocked on the door. Emily gestured for him to enter.

He dipped his head. "Dinner is now available in the dining car should you wish to eat."

With unexpected spryness, the elderly couple scrambled to their feet. Madame Vidal clung to her husband's arm. "Excellent. Do you know what they're serving, young man?"

An apologetic smile on his face, he shook his head. "Non, but unfortunately whatever it is will not be haute cuisine."

"No matter." Madame Vidal smoothed her skirt. "As long as the food is edible, and with Germans on the train, it just may be." She turned to Emily. "Will you join us?"

"We—"

"Perhaps, shortly." Gerard interrupted Emily, and she glanced at his stony profile.

"*À bientôt*. See you soon." The couple exited the compartment, the lingering scent of the woman's floral perfume still in the air.

Emily flopped against the padded bench. "I thought they would never leave. Do you think they bought our story?"

"Hard to tell. Seems like it." He frowned. "I think we should consider getting off the train before we pull into the next station. Could be dicey. We'd have to leap at just the right moment, when we've slowed on the approach, but not so late as to be seen by the brakeman." His eyes darkened and seemed to caress her face. "You could get hurt. I wouldn't want that."

She blinked. Oh, that he cared what happened to her like a husband would for his wife. No, she was imagining things. He was simply being a good senior agent. "Worse than parachuting from a plane?"

He chuckled. "Probably not. And I think you're quite capable of the jump, but with every mission we need to weigh the risks." He winked. "Besides, I don't want to have to cart you across the country if you break a leg."

Her insides flipped, and she swatted his arm. "I don't want to have to carry *you*. We've got too far to go."

His face lit up as his chuckle turned into a full-fledged guffaw. "As much as I'd enjoy that, let's assume neither of us gets injured."

Despite the danger, his jaw had lost its tenseness, and his eyes sparkled. The banter seemed to have taken the edge off his stress. He ribbed her and treated her with respect, as if she were an intelligent colleague. He also seemed to go out of his way to protect her without being overbearing or misogynistic. When was the last time someone in her life had considered her an equal?

Not at work, and certainly not at home. She gazed out the window. Did he feel the electricity that periodically crackled between them?

He cleared his throat. "All kidding aside, I think we need to get off the train and return to the original plan of hiking toward the border, with or without the Resistance. We no longer have the radio, and our identities seem to have been compromised. We're pushing our luck by traveling in public."

"I agree. The thirty minutes with that couple was exhausting. I'm still not sure they're as unassuming as we're supposed to believe, and the fewer times I have to pretend to be someone I'm not, the better. Do you think we'll be able to find a cell to help us?"

"It will take some doing, but I believe it's possible. We can start with churches. From what I've seen, many of the country's clergy do not agree with the Nazis' tactics or with the Vichy government. That doesn't mean they're in the Resistance, but they may know things or have contacts."

"Good idea. I'll pray God gives us guidance." She finger-combed her hair and frowned. "Perhaps the minister could tell us where we can secure a bath. I'm a mess."

"Try being on maneuvers for weeks at a time. It's a wonder the enemy can't smell troops coming." His eyes flashed. "You're lovely, but I would appreciate the opportunity to clean up, too."

"And you're a sweetheart for saying that." She grinned, and her heart sped up. If he continued to compliment her, she'd begin to believe he felt something for her. She crossed her ankles, and her foot caught a scrap of paper lying on the floor. "What's this?" She leaned forward and grabbed the sheet. Her body went cold, then sweat sprang out along her hairline as she stared at a sketch of her face and Gerard's that could only have been drawn in the last few days.

His intake of breath was sharp, and he pointed to the announcement below the pictures. "Wanted for treason. Considered armed and dangerous. Contact the authorities with any information. Reward: 20,000 reichsmarks. There's no maybe about it. This flyer proves we're being pursued and are most likely compromised."

Emily's mouth went dry. "Did the Vidals drop this or leave it on purpose as a warning to us? Was it already on the floor when we arrived? I don't remember seeing it before they entered the compartment. Do you?"

"No. The poster clinches it. We need to get off the train immediately and take our chances in the countryside. Who knows how many of these leaflets have been distributed. We also need to figure out how to change our appearance again. Your hair is already shorter, but perhaps you should cut it even closer to your head." He frowned and fingered a stray lock hanging by her cheek. "Bad enough we had to bleach your beautiful cinnamon-colored hair, but to chop it off seems a crime."

She stilled under his touch, and her breath hitched. Did he have any idea how he affected her? At least it took her mind off being on a wanted poster. She wiped damp palms on her slacks. "Uh...we should appear more ragged and poor. Our clothes are that of simple villagers, but they are only slightly worn. We are less likely to be bothered if we're dirty and foul smelling."

He rubbed his hands together. "Excellent idea. What do you have in mind?"

"If we pass a farm, we could find something *earthy* from the fields. That would definitely be off putting. If not, rubbing rotten food from someone's refuse pile on our clothes might work. I don't relish either choice, but…" She shrugged. "What do you think?"

"I'd rather be outdoors than anywhere else, so the farm *motif* is my preference. Easier to obtain, too."

She nodded. "Farm life it is. How much farther until the next stop?"

Gerard glanced at his watch. "About three hours, which means darkness will be falling, making for good cover. We should eat, but I don't want to expose ourselves more than necessary, so going to the dining car is out. Others may have seen the flyer." He looked at her, his brow furrowed. "Can you hold up without a meal?"

"Her stomach grumbled, and she giggled. "Believe it or not, yes I can."

His lips quirked in a smile. "Good girl."

The door rattled.

He pulled her to him and put his mouth close to her ear. "They're back. Follow my lead. It is imperative that this couple believe we are newlyweds and not Resistance members."

Before she could respond, Gerard drew back and looked deep into her eyes, then laid a kiss on her right cheek, his lips warm and full of promise. He kissed her left cheek and then her forehead. His fingers kneaded her back. Tingles danced up her spine, and she shivered. Time stood still as he lowered his head and pressed his lips to hers, soft yet insistent. He deepened the kiss, his breath mingling with hers. She closed her eyes, losing herself in his embrace. Tremors crashed over her in waves. A moan escaped, and her mind emptied of all thought. Then she was kissing him in return.

A cough.

Gerard continued to explore her mouth.

Another cough. Louder.

He pulled back and bumped the tip of her nose with his.

Her eyes flew open. The world tilted, then righted itself. Face heating, she dipped her head. She'd acted the part of a floozy, a loose woman, despite the fact they were supposedly married. They were married, even if only on paper. Would the couple be suitably shocked yet convinced by their behavior? She couldn't meet the woman's gaze that burned in her direction.

"Our apologies." Gerard ran a hand over his head and seemed to be affecting embarrassment. "My *maman et papa* taught me better. They would be disappointed with me, but I was overcome with love for my wife. With passion. Surely, you understand."

Emily looked up, her breathing ragged. "Oui. Forgive us."

Monsieur Vidal thrust out his chest. "We may be old, but we are not *mort*. However, you must control yourself when in public. Your behavior is most unseemly, even for a Frenchman." His mouth twisted. "We came to bid you *bonne nuit*, but it appears we shouldn't have bothered. Best wishes to you."

Madame Vidal drew herself to her full height. "We will not see you again before we disembark. Godspeed."

Emily's gaze shot to the woman. Godspeed? Had He sent the couple?

An imperceptible nod from the elderly woman, then her husband led her from the carriage.

Gerard grinned; his face flushed. "I feel like I've just been to the principal's office, but it appears he may have believed our little performance. Otherwise, we would not have received the reprimand." He nudged her shoulder. "You were great. Very authentic."

Mouth throbbing, Emily nodded and pressed her lips together. Right. A performance. How had she forgotten that? The realism of his kiss, that's how. Stupid to let her emotions take over. She could not allow that to happen. Once they escaped to England, they would go their separate ways. Her heart shrank, and she blinked back tears.

Chapter Twenty-One

Gerard peered out the compartment window at the dusky shadows on the landscape. Finally. Enough darkness to make their attempt to jump from the train. The last three hours had been an excruciating wait in alternating silence and awkward conversation. He'd pulled the curtains on the glass panel in the door to prevent nosy passengers looking in, but the fabric covers also meant he didn't have a view either.

The muscles in his back ached from being clenched in anticipation of discovery. He massaged his shoulders and rotated his neck in an effort to get relief, but the knots under his skin remained firmly in place.

Next to him, Emily sat with her head bowed and eyes closed. Fingers laced together, her knuckles were white. If she was praying, her conversation with the Almighty didn't seem to be bringing her any peace. The glass panes reflected the soft angles of her face, and he resisted the urge to trace a line down her jaw where her ear met the curve of her neck.

He pulled up the sleeve on his coat and checked his watch. "It's time." Rising, he buttoned his jacket then dug into his bag for his knitted wool cap.

Emily's eyes opened, and she nodded, lines of fatigue etched on her face. She climbed to her feet, grabbing her satchel and tossing it on the bench. One by one she pulled out articles of clothing and put them on. "Too bad it's not winter when I'd be carrying bulky sweaters and coats." A wry smile smoothed her expression.

"All you gals want to be thin. See, there are benefits to being…uh…more rounded."

"You'd think considering all the potatoes we've eaten since arriving in France I would be." She patted her flat middle. "Hopefully, my clothes will do the trick."

Gerard eyed her figure, now swathed in layers and began to peel off his jacket. "Put this on."

"No, you need the padding, too. Remember, I'm not going to carry you if you bust a leg or twist an ankle."

He snorted a laugh.

Her eyes sparkled, and she grinned. "Let's get this over with." Uncertainty crossed her face. "Okay, Mr. Instructor-partner, let's review technique. I've only got one chance to do this correctly."

"It's best to jump while the train is either slowing or moving uphill, and according to the map the approach to the next station has a curved hill, forcing the train to slow down. We should scan the area for debris, so we don't land on anything that can injure us. A grassy area is ideal, and I think we may be good there. This area of France isn't known to be too rocky."

Elbows bent, he pressed his arms to the side of his skull. "Be sure to cradle that pretty, little head of yours to prevent getting knocked out.

Your landing form should be similar to that of parachuting. Roll onto one shoulder then into a ball. Not like a somersault."

She squatted. "I start out like this, right?"

"Yes. That will give you the best trajectory as you leap away from the train. Be sure to jump perpendicular to the car so your momentum doesn't carry you toward the wheels or the tracks."

"Okay." She gave him a thumbs-up and huffed out a loud breath. "Another skill to add to my résumé for after the war." She tapped her finger on her chin. "Oh wait. I can't tell anyone I was running for my life in France, so I had to jump off a moving train. It would be more fun if I could keep the incident in my repertoire of stories."

He snickered. "You can tell me all about it. I promise to be impressed."

"Yeah, it's not really the same, but thanks."

"Follow me, Madame Boucher. We'll jump from the connection between the cars." Before he could change his mind, he pulled her to him and placed a quick kiss on her forehead. Her skin was warm under his lips. "For luck."

Her eyes widened.

Releasing her, he slid open the wooden door and moved into the aisle, Emily close on his heels. At the end of the car, he shoved open the hatch. Wind whooshed past, and he ducked his head. He stepped onto the jostling, metal platform and planted his feet against the motion. His heart pounded, and sweat slicked his palms. A chasm separated the training manual from his current reality. Had the bloke who wrote the chapter actually performed the act?

"I'll go first," Emily shouted above the clanking of the couplings. "If I see what it's like for you, I might lose my nerve, and I don't want to be stuck on this contraption full of Nazis."

"Don't lollygag. I won't either."

Her face pale, she grabbed the railing and crouched, her eyes closed for a brief moment.

Gerard squeezed her shoulder. *Dear God, please keep her from injury.* He held his breath.

Eyes wide, she cradled her head and launched herself from the train. She landed on a sandy embankment three or four yards away from the tracks.

The door to the carriage opened, and he vaulted off the platform. His body slammed into the ground. Rolling. Rolling. He grunted at each contact with the hard soil then came to stop.

*"Halt! Hände hoch oder ich schieße."*

He lifted his head and looked toward the receding train. A uniformed figure of an SS soldier pointed his gun in their direction, a scowl twisting his features. They'd jumped none too soon.

The train rounded the curve and disappeared from view.

Muffled footsteps sounded. He grabbed for his pistol and turned.

Emily limped toward him, her satchel hanging from one shoulder. A triumphant smile lit her dusty face.

He returned her smile. "We're alive, but you're hurt."

"Not seriously. Just tweaked my ankle a bit. I'll wrap it before we go." She knelt by his side. A quick intake of breath, then she caught her lower lip in her teeth. "What about you?"

"Black and blue by tonight, no doubt, but otherwise okay. We've got to get out of here. One of the SS men saw us."

"Oh, no."

"Yeah." He climbed to his feet, muscles screaming with each movement. "He's probably already got a call into the next station to be on the lookout, so let's bypass the village and head straight for Paris."

"What do you think he knows?"

Gerard hiked one shoulder. "Hard to say, but the fact that we got off the train in such an...uh...unorthodox manner makes us appear guilty. I'm not sure he saw you or whether he'd be able to recognize me, but I suggest we ditch these clothes as soon as possible and assume your guise of looking poor and haggard."

A dog barked within the trees, and Gerard whirled, hand on his gun. His stomach roiled. Were the Germans already searching for them?

Rustling. A whistle. Bushes moved, and a boy of perhaps ten years old emerged from the woods, his walking stick gripped in a gloved hand. Behind him, a large, shaggy dog appeared, tongue lolling. Leaves clung to the canine's heavy, white coat.

Gerard sagged and stuffed his weapon into his waistband. "*Salut.* Your dog is beautiful. Is he friendly?"

"Oui." The boy nodded. "Are you lost?"

"Non. We are on our honeymoon." Gerard held out his hand, palm down. The dog trotted over, sniffed his fingers then licked them before turning his attention to Emily.

With a tilt to his head, the youngster narrowed his eyes. "Why are you wearing so many of your clothes?"

"Well…"

Emily stepped forward with a smile and stroked the dog's head. "It's a long story. One I'll tell you if you help us out. Do you live far from here?"

"Just through those trees. I come to watch the train every day, but Maman had extra chores for me, so I was late. That's when I saw you jump off the train. Do you not have a ticket? My older brother used to do that. He liked trying to pull one over on the conductor."

"He sounds smart, too. Why isn't he with you?"

The boy's face fell. "We haven't seen him since the Germans came to our town. Phillipe is fourteen, so they put him to work in the labor camps. Maman cries at night when she thinks I'm asleep."

"And your father?"

"He died when I was a baby."

Gerard's chest tightened. Children forced to grow up too soon. What other sorrows had this boy experienced? He held out his hand. "I'm Jules, and this is my wife, Sophie. What's your name?"

"Pierre."

"Is your maman home?"

"Yes, we did school this morning, but she sent me outside so she could get her chores done."

"You don't attend school in your village?"

Pierre shook his head. "No, the teacher is gone. I don't know where. Our village is mostly women now. Not too many men are there, just the *grandpères*." He snapped his fingers, and the dog ran to his side. "Follow me. I will take you home. Then we can tell Maman how you jumped from the train."

"Well—"

Emily ruffled Pierre's hair. "I bet you didn't tell her about your brother. Some things are best left as secrets."

"You're right. She would have worried, so I never said anything. I'm good at keeping secrets." He held out his hand, and Emily grasped it. They headed into the foliage.

Gerard's heart tugged. Emily claimed she had no maternal instincts, yet she'd created a bond with Pierre almost immediately, otherwise the child would not have reached out to her, not in these days of subterfuge and suspicion.

What would it be like to raise a family with her? To wake up every morning to her smiling face? To approach each day with her by his side? He scrubbed at his face with cold hands then followed their trail. Somewhere along the journey, he'd fallen in love with his student-partner. He didn't want to annul their marriage when they returned to the States.

What would the OSS think about that? Would they have to give up their positions, or would the organization separate their assignments? Too many questions for which he had no answers.

Fifteen minutes later, they arrived at a tiny, tired-looking cottage nestled among the trees. Pierre released Emily's hand and skipped toward the house. "Maman, I am home and brought some new friends."

The door opened. A petite, thirtysomething woman appeared, her expression guarded. Her straw-colored hair was swept up on her head, and a smudge of flour graced her cheek. A floral apron covered her light-blue cotton dress.

Emily dipped her head. "*Bonne journée.* We mean you or Pierre no harm. We're travelers. May we come inside to rest and get a cup of water?"

With trembling hands, the woman reached into her apron pocket. She pulled out a piece of paper and held it up.

A leaflet identical to the one on the train. Gerard's stomach clenched. The authorities had lost no time in spreading the word about them. Was the net closing in? How much time did they have before the SS started sniffing around? He would do everything in his power to evade the Germans. He and Emily would be tortured if captured, and he could not let that happen to her. Not while there was breath in his body.

## Chapter Twenty-Two

Emily's heart dropped. Would she and Gerard successfully elude the Nazis or did Pierre's mother plan to report them? The woman's expression held a mixture of fear and determination. Did she hope to collect the reward? Her flimsy dress and apron contained no telltale bulges hiding weapons.

"We mean you no harm," Emily repeated. "My husband and I...there's been a misunderstanding. Can you help us?" She held her hands in the air in surrender and jerked her head at Gerard in an attempt to entice him to do the same. Seconds later, his arms rose, and she blew out a deep breath.

"*S'il vous plaît.* We just need some water, and a change of clothes." Gerard voice was low and soothing.

"Maman, why don't you say something?" Pierre hopped up and down on one foot. "They are my new friends. Don't you like them?"

His mother's gaze slid from her son to Emily. After what seemed a lifetime, she stuffed the paper in her pocket and beckoned for them to follow her inside the cottage.

Emily's knees nearly buckled with relief. She hitched up the satchel on her shoulder and held out her hand to Pierre. The youngster grabbed her fingers and skipped beside her. She grinned, his behavior lifting her heart.

Gerard clomped into the room behind her.

She knew without looking that he surveyed the home looking for clues about the family and their allegiance. Worn but clean, upholstered living room furniture clustered at one end of the large room. The other end held a plain, wooden table and four chairs. Nestled between the two areas, the kitchen held a stainless steel sink, tiny stove, and an even smaller icebox.

Still silent, the woman opened a cabinet and retrieved two glasses. She cranked the pump handle at the counter, and water dribbled into the cups.

Pierre pulled out one of the kitchen chairs. "You should sit down. Then you can tell Maman all about your adventure." His eyes widened, and he clamped a hand over his mouth as if realizing he'd almost broken his promise not to say anything about them jumping from the train.

His mother pivoted and set the glasses on the table with a thump then stroked Pierre's hair. "Son, let them rest from your chattering." A tentative smile flitted across her face. "He is alone much of the time. He misses his friends."

Emily lowered herself onto the seat and drank deeply. "Merci. He is a good boy. You should be proud of him."

"Oui." She wrapped her arms around her middle. "Please be honest. Has there truly been a misunderstanding, or are you on the run from our occupiers?"

Inexplicable peace settled over Emily. Was God telling her she could trust Pierre's mother? She couldn't share too much information, but perhaps a kernel of truth would assuage the woman's suspicions and build a bridge. "There is no misunderstanding."

Gerard gasped then pressed his lips together, his face dark.

"It's okay." Emily pitched her voice to a whisper. "She won't give us up."

"How do you know? The Nazis can be very *persuasive*."

She laid her hand on his arm. "I just know. Please bear with me on this."

He studied her face for a long moment then nodded. "For now."

"Fine." She turned back to Pierre's mother. "We need to make contact with *La Résistance.* As you see from the flyer, we must get out of the country. The Germans have us in their sights and seemed determine to find us. Can you provide clothes? We want to look like beggars."

"I can do better than that. Come." She entered a small room that held two single beds separated by a large dresser. She gestured to Gerard. "Please help me move this."

"Pierre and I can do it, can't we, little man?"

The youngster executed a serious salute. "Oui, monsieur."

With Gerard doing most of the work, they scooted the heavy piece of furniture away from the wall.

Pierre's mother knelt and removed the floorboards revealing an ancient-looking trunk. She unlatched the lid and withdrew a case beneath which was a jumble of wigs and clothing.

"Goodness." Emily's breath exploded. "You're not part of the local theater troupe, are you?"

"Non." She smirked. "Well, not anymore, but my skills have proven useful." With efficient motions, she rifled through the items and pulled out several articles of tattered clothing and a long, blonde wig before closing the lid and replacing the floor boards. "Quickly, you must change. Then I will do your makeup, and we can get you on your way. I received word this morning the Germans are sweeping the entire province. You must have done something very bad for them to be this tenacious in their search."

"We left a Vichy police officer dead."

Her eyes rounded. "That would do it. Please return the bureau to its place." She hurried from the room and closed the door behind her.

Emily snatched the clothes from the bed. "Uh…"

"We've no time for modesty. I will turn my back, and you do the same. Our hostess is correct. We must waste no time. The Germans could be here at any time."

Her face heating, she nodded then kicked off her shoes before pivoting on her heel. She peeled off the layers of shirts, and the air chilled her skin. She removed all but one pair of slacks and drew the dress over her head. Shapeless and stained, it draped over her like a potato sack. She pushed her feet into the scuffed boots, surprised to discover they fit perfectly.

Behind her, the sound of rustling stopped. Gerard must have finished dressing. "I'm ready. Are you?"

"Yes."

She turned, and her jaw dropped. Too-short brown twill pants were cinched to his more than six-foot frame, with a rope belt. A few inches of hairy legs were exposed above the tops of his equally scuffed boots. The matching brown shirt was ill-fitting and torn. A ragged blanket hung on his shoulders, and a slouch hat was pulled low on his forehead. If it weren't for his riveting blue eyes, she might overlook him in a crowd. "You're transformed." She put her hands on her hips. "Except for your expression. You need to look less...uh..."

His lips quirked. "Like a man on a mission?"

A giggle escaped. "Yes. You're still scouring the room."

"How's this." His gaze took on a vacuous stare, and the left corner of his mouth drooped.

"Wow. Much better. You could have a career in Hollywood when this is all over."

"Yeah, that's how I want to spend my days." He shook his head then grinned. "Pierre's mother is going to have her work cut out. Despite the shabby appearance of your outfit, you're too lovely. The Jerrys will never believe you're a homeless, helpless Frenchwoman."

Her toes curled, and she nibbled her lower lip. He thought she was attractive. "Yes, well, that's one man's opinion." She folded her discarded clothes, lifted a couple of floorboards, and then tucked the items into the cubbyhole. Focus, Emily. Just because he thinks you're pretty doesn't mean he has feelings for you. She forced a smile and climbed to her feet. "I'll be in the living room, Hercules. Hide your stuff before you put back the dresser."

He chuckled.

Her heart skittered. If she didn't get a grip on her emotions, the entire mission to escape could be in jeopardy. She left the room on heavy feet.

"Ah, good. Now, sit. I will do something with that beautiful face of yours."

The second time in two minutes, she'd been referred to as good looking. Emily frowned. They'd obviously never seen her sister Cora, the one whose appearance turned heads everywhere she went. As Pierre's mother dabbed cosmetics on her skin, Emily closed her eyes.

"Voilà. You are *finie*."

"Much better," Gerard's voice rumbled.

Emily's eyes flew open. "Ugly enough for you." She clambered from the chair.

"Never." His eyes shuttered as he lowered himself on the seat. "I'm assuming you know how to make me appear dirty, not wearing cosmetics."

The woman dipped her head. "My abilities have not failed me yet." Seconds later, he was nearly unrecognizable.

The unmistakable thunder of a vehicle sounded outside.

Heart pounding, Emily froze. Very few people owned cars except the authorities.

Gerard sprang into action. "Put the cosmetic case in a closet, and pray they don't choose to search the premises. Emily, you lie down and pretend to be ill. I'll sit by your side and look distraught."

Emily swallowed against the nausea that roiled in her stomach. It wouldn't be difficult to act the part. She hurried to the sofa and stretched out on the lumpy cushions. Pierre's mother raced into the room with a shabby blanket, and Gerard laid it over Emily's body. She wrapped her arms around herself under the scratchy wool fabric. The woman's makeup abilities were about to be put to the test, especially if Sturmbannführer Krause was part of the group.

Heavy knocking sounded at the door. "Open the door."

"*Un moment.*" Pierre's mother wiped her hands down her skirt then straightened her spine. She walked across the small space and opened the door.

Three gestapo officers strode into the house.

Cracking an eyelid, Emily nearly wept in relief. Krause was not among the haughty, twentysomething-year-old men. She and Gerard were not out of the woods, but their chances had increased by his absence.

The shortest of the trio, a bulldog of a man, pointed at Emily. "What is wrong with her?"

Gerard sniffled. "I'm afraid it might be influenza. Her symptoms came on quickly. We've not had chance to send for the doctor."

"Influenza?" The man stepped back and held his hand up to his mouth. "This house should be quarantined." He narrowed his eyes at Gerard. "Why are you here? You look healthy enough to me. Why are you not fighting for with the Vichy der führer?"

"I am on leave from the factory where I work. My maman died, and I was given time to attend her funeral. On the way back, we decided to get married, because life is too short. This morning my wife took ill. I'm so worried."

"She doesn't look sick to me."

Emily broke into a paroxysm of coughing. Her throat burned as she faked the attack. Would the nasty man believe her or at least be so put off by her possible contagion, he'd leave?

Gerard dabbed at her forehead with his handkerchief.

Through her shirt, goose bumps formed at his touch. Her face warmed. Hopefully, the officer would interpret her blush as part of her sickness.

The wiry officer leaned toward Bulldog. "Sir, perhaps it would be best if we moved on. You don't want to be infected, do you?"

"Nein, but this could be a performance for our benefit. You two search the house, and I will check their papers."

"Jawohl." They headed to the bedroom where bumps and thuds were soon heard.

The man held out his hand, palm up. "Your identity cards, marriage certificate, and travel papers."

"Oui, monsieur." Gerard jumped to his feet and grabbed his rucksack. He retrieved the requested documents and held them out to the officer.

He snatched them from Gerard's grasp and scanned the contents. His head jerked up. "It seems you've found favor with us. Mayor Reneau signed your license and Standartenführer Weber issued your visas. Impressive. You don't look important enough to warrant their attention. How did this come about?"

"Quite fortuitously, monsieur." With a shrug and downcast eyes, Gerard explained what happened at the wedding.

Emily pulled the blanket closer to her chin and sipped from the glass that Pierre's mother had set by her side during the commotion. The tepid liquid soothed her dry mouth and trickled down her parched throat. *Please, Lord, work this out so that we might escape.*

The officer returned the papers and peered at Emily as his underlings entered the room. "Nothing in the bedroom, sir. Would you like us to search the rest of the house?"

He shook his head. "We're finished here." He swung his gaze to Gerard. "I suggest you see to your wife and get a doctor here immediately. Influenza is deadly. You must love her very much to risk your life by caring for her."

"I do. She is everything to me." Gerard tucked a stray lock of hair behind Emily's ear.

She shivered. Nestled under his arm, she believed his words. He couldn't possibly mean them, but she did. Somewhere during their days together, she'd fallen in love with him. She would never tell him, because he'd think her foolish, but she felt a security she'd never experienced. Whatever happened with the Germans or their attempt to flee France didn't matter. She would be with Gerard, and they would face the danger together. Separation when they returned to the States would be excruciating, but she would cherish the memories of their time together in her heart. Her broken heart.

## Chapter Twenty-Three

Gerard glanced at his watch. "It's been three hours since the German goons left. I believe it's safe for us to continue our journey." He rose from the sofa and faced Pierre's mother. He clasped her hands. "Thank you for risking your life for us. For everything you've done. Is there anything we can do for you before we leave?"

"Non. I will pray for your safe travels. Do I need to review the instructions on how to find the café?"

He shook his head. "I remember."

Pierre ran across the room and wrapped his arms around Gerard's leg. "I will miss you. Thank you for making Maman smile again, even if only for a little while."

"And I will miss you." Gerard swallowed the lump in his throat. The bright, inquisitive boy had wormed his way into Gerard's heart. He ruffled the youngster's hair. "Take good care of your maman."

The boy sniffled and nodded then released Gerard. He hugged Emily before returning to his mother's side.

Emily embraced Pierre's mother. "Words cannot express our appreciation. May God bless you and keep you in His arms." She picked up her satchel and slung it over her shoulder. "Ready."

They exited the cottage that had been their refuge, and his heart constricted. *Please, God, don't let anything happen to this small family. Place Your hedge of protection around them while they do their part in fighting the evil in this land.*

"You okay?" Emily cocked her head.

"Yeah. It's one thing to be with other soldiers who risk their lives in combat, but to see civilians…women and children…choose to put their lives on the line…to see ordinary people perform extraordinary acts like that. Admiration doesn't begin to describe my feelings, you know?"

"You're a good man, Gerard." Her face glowed.

If only she knew the atrocities he'd committed upon ordinary people in the context of war. No need to tell her.

He dipped low in an exaggerated bow. "At last, recognition of my gentlemanly traits. Now, daylight is fading. We need to make up for the time lost entertaining the Germans."

She giggled and executed an exaggerated curtsy. "I am at your command, sir."

They set off at a fast walk, Gerard's gaze ricocheting across the landscape. The muscles in his neck and shoulders tightened. Should they have waited until full darkness to travel? Was tramping down the country lane less suspicious than skulking behind bushes? Chipmunks darted between the shrubs while birds chirped in the tree branches overhead. As long as the winged creatures were singing, trouble was far away. Wasn't it?

Thirty minutes passed; Emily walked beside him in silence. She lifted her face to the sky and sighed.

He raised an eyebrow. "Yes?"

"Please refrain from laughing when I say these last few weeks have been like nothing I've ever experienced. I don't mean being a radio operator. Interacting with these people…seeing them try to survive under occupation. Choosing to resist." She tugged at the straps on her bag. "I lived with the French people during my year abroad and realized they are just like Americans. They want to fall in love, get married, raise a family, and have a job they enjoy. But now, it is a day-to-day struggle, one in which they could die. Yet they keep fighting." She met his eyes. "My life will never be the same."

"Nor mine." He pointed to a copse of ash trees where a pair of triangles was carved in the trunk. Did the Germans ever notice these signs? Would he and Emily find an SS soldier or two at the end of the trail? "This is our turnoff."

She nodded and entered the woods. "And I've said this before, but I didn't picture myself running for my life through another country."

"It's probably a good thing we don't know what's in store for us. Don't you think?"

"Perhaps if I knew what to expect, I'd second-guess myself less often."

He frowned. "We'll get that trained out of you yet. I'm sorry you've grown used to the negative voices in your ear. You are an intelligent and courageous woman. How many of your friends or family members have signed up to be an undercover agent? I'd hazard the answer is none of them."

They continued to tramp for nearly an hour. He stopped and squinted through the foliage. "There. I think I see the boulder we've been looking for. The size of a tank with one side sheared off." The tightness in his chest eased. He hadn't gotten them lost. Had Francoise been able to arrange for contact from *La Rèsistance* as promised?

Gerard cleared his throat then emitted the metallic-sounding, vibrating call of the nightjar, one of the birds Europe that sing at dusk. Seconds later, an identical call filtered toward them from the other side of the stone. He repeated the song, and again it echoed.

Movement. Then a shadowy figure emerged from behind the trees and approached. Tall and lanky, the man was dressed entirely in black with a beret set on his head at a jaunty angle—the first of their two identification signals, since wearing the French icon was forbidden. The man put his hand over his heart. "I love the sounds of birds at night."

Emily mimicked his action, then responded in a whisper. "Only that of the nightjar."

"Bon. This way. Stay close to me as the terrain is uneven."

The last time a guide had said that, Emily ended up rolling down a hillside. Gerard bit back a retort. Hopefully, this journey would be less eventful. Time crawled as they trudged through underbrush, shrubs, and trees. He cast an eye at the moon over his right shoulder. They headed due south without wavering.

His legs ached, and the bottoms of his feet burned. How was Emily faring? He squeezed her shoulder.

She turned and smiled, her teeth flashing.

Still hanging on apparently. The girl...no, woman, was indefatigable. He'd love a chance to tell her family. He blinked and shook the thought aside.

More time passed, and the forest thinned.

Their escort held up his hand. "We have arrived. Wait here for approximately an hour, maybe a little more. The train will come, chugging at minimal speed because of the incline of the tracks. The door on the second to last freight car will be open. Climb inside and ride until the engine slows again at the next slope. Jump off and travel east for two miles until you come to a small village. Enter the Café Pâtisserie and order a beignet, saying you wish you could have a dozen. Your contact will be wearing a green turban and matching sash. Godspeed."

"Merci."

The man bowed and vanished through the trees.

"Might as well make ourselves comfortable." Gerard shed his pack and sat on the ground. "I don't know about you, but I could use a rest."

"I'd love to remove my boots, but I might never get them back on." Emily dropped beside him. "I'm exhausted, yet my senses are on high alert. The alternating boredom and terrorizing fright are wearing me down. I may sleep for a week when we get back to England."

He chuckled. "Me, too. Hopefully that will be enough to overcome the fatigue. What will you do after that?"

"Providing I don't get sent on another assignment immediately, I'd like to do something frivolous." She shrugged, bumping his shoulder. "Shopping holds no allure, well, clothes anyway. I can lose myself in a bookstore."

"Then you'll love Hatchards. The bookshop was founded in the early eighteenth century."

"Which means they've survived other wars. Impressive."

"Agreed. Then what will you do?"

He felt her turn in the inky blackness, but he kept his gaze averted.

"Why all the questions?"

"We've got time to kill, need to stay awake, and it's too dark for tic-tac-toe."

Emily snorted a laugh. "Point taken." She sat up straight. "Okay, here's my fantasy for when we return. After I've slept for a week, of course."

"Of course."

"I'll take a steaming hot bath with a tub full of water. I don't know how the British stand it, with their tepid water only four inches deep. Anyway, then I want to stuff myself full of food that is not potatoes or turnips. Perhaps prepare a nice, juicy steak. After that, I'm going to park on an overstuffed sofa and read until my eyes spin. I might go for a walk in Hyde Park, but that may seem too much like the trekking we've been doing. Finally, I'll take a nap. Boring, huh?"

"I'll take boring any day."

"No, you won't, but thanks for saying." She sighed. "I wanted excitement. Little did I know…" Tension colored her voice, and she repositioned herself, jostling his arm.

Warmth from her body permeated his jacket, and he fought the desire to draw her into his arms, to tell her everything would be all right, and they could handle anything together. But that too was a fantasy.

A light pierced the night, and the ground vibrated. He jumped up. The train was earlier than anticipated. Did its arrival portend good or bad?

He bent to help Emily rise, but she'd already scrambled to her feet. "Why is the train already here?"

"I wonder the same thing. The Germans pride themselves on adhering to a timely schedule. Perhaps too soon is better than too late."

She lifted her rucksack and slung it over her shoulder. "Guess there's one way to find out."

Rocking and shimmying, the rumbling locomotive trundled past their position. The churning clickety-clack of the wheels slowed, and Gerard nudged Emily. "It won't be long now."

Hunched over, they crept toward the tracks then trotted alongside the train.

Five cars. Four cars. Three cars. Two cars. As promised, the door on the next carriage stood open. What or who was inside? His heart skittered. *Please God, let this work.*

"Go." His hiss split the air.

He threw himself toward the yawning cavity, and his body slammed against the floor of the car with a grunt.

Emily landed beside him, her legs hanging over the edge. She rolled to her side and groaned. Clutching her knee, she whimpered.

"You're injured." He bolted upright then bent over her, his hands hovering above her leg. "How bad is the pain? Do you think it's a sprain, or did you break it?"

With eyes squeezed shut, she moaned. "I'm not sure. It feels like there's a knife sticking into my knee cap." Her voice was thin. "With any luck, it's only bruised, but if not, you should leave me behind, I'll—"

"Absolutely not. We are leaving this country *together.* No argument."

In the dim moonlight, a crooked grin split her face, and she opened her eyes. "What about your threat not to carry me if I sprained an ankle or busted a leg?"

His breath expelled in a whoosh as he snickered. Once again, she'd proven she was a strong, resilient woman. He couldn't let anything happen to her. He wouldn't. "I need to examine your injury. Do you want a silver bullet to bite on?"

"No, but thanks for the offer. How well did you do on the first-aid course?"

"Well enough. Now, lie still while I see how bad the damage is."

"The good news is I won't have to pretend to be a cripple, but the bad news is I will slow us down." She closed her eyes and laid her head on the floor.

He tugged up her pant leg to bare her knee. He pulled out his flashlight and cupped one hand around the bulb before clicking on the power. He held the beam close. Already beginning to discolor in shades of black and blue, the puffy joint was crisscrossed with abrasions. He prodded the knee. Warm, but not hot. A good sign. He moved the leg side to side.

A swift intake of breath escaped Emily's lips, but she didn't cry out.

"Your knee doesn't appear to be broken, and the swelling is minimal, so you may only have a slight sprain. You banged it up pretty good, so it's going to hurt for a while. Let me wrap it in case you did twist the muscles or ligaments."

"Thank you, *Doctor.* You're my hero.*"

"Funny." His chest swelled. She was obviously being sarcastic, but her words bathed his weary soul in pride. He liked the idea of being her hero. Too bad that would end when they reached England.

## Chapter Twenty-Four

Emily shifted on the hard floor, and pain radiated up her leg. She pressed her lips together, holding her breath. How could she continue with a bum limb? Gerard must be disgusted with her. She'd repeatedly messed up their mission, and now she was impacting their ability to get home because of her injury.

The train slowed, its wheels squealing against the tracks. No time to dwell on her situation. Their moment to disembark had arrived. She took a deep breath and climbed to her feet, swallowing a groan as her knee protested at the movement.

Gerard wrapped his arm around her shoulder. "Let me go first, then I'll catch you."

She nodded. Landing was the least of her worries. Rather, the miles-long hike to their next stop crowded her thoughts.

Chugging at a crawl, the steam-powered monster inched up the slope.

"I'll jog alongside and stick the flashlight in my jacket so you can see me. Jump toward me on the count of three."

"Okay."

In a blur, he disappeared through the opening. A second later, his voice broke though the darkness. One…two…three!"

She threw herself toward the sound. Hanging in the air, time stood still. Then she was in his arms, his musky smell of sweat, hay, and outdoors permeating her senses. Wrapped in his embrace, they tumbled and rolled on the ground.

"Good girl." A smile laced his words.

Her heart swelled. Success. She hadn't fallen, or worse, hurt him in the process. *Thank You, God.*

He helped her stand. "Are you okay to walk?"

"I have to be." She put her weight on the injured leg. A dull ache pulsed in her muscles. Her eyes widened. "Yes. My knee no longer feels like someone is sticking knives or needles into it. Resting has helped."

In the distance, the train reached the top of the incline and rounded the bend. Silence fell.

"Excellent, but we must be careful not to overdo." Gerard retrieved his flashlight, shone the ray on his compass, and then clicked off the light. He pointed east. "Best get moving. We should be there in a couple of hours."

They walked to the tree line that edged the meadow. Pitch dark or not, walking across the middle of the expanse was foolish. Their feet sank into the soft ground. Deep in the woods, an owl hooted. Even deeper, another answered. Bats chattered and pirouetted in the sky.

Emily stuffed her hands into her pockets and tried to ignore the throbbing in her knee. Snippets of her favorite hymns floated through her head, and the tension slipped from her shoulders. After an hour, they rested, then continued on their way. Wiping the perspiration along her hairline, she plucked at her blouse that stuck to her skin. Would she ever be clean again?

Gerard stopped and pointed at the collection of cottages about a hundred yards away.

She drew alongside him, and her chin lifted. They'd reached the village in good time. She hadn't slowed them down. "It won't be light for another few hours, so we should be able to slip in undetected."

"As long as no one is lying in wait for us."

"Surely, they can't have staked out every village within a hundred-mile radius."

He shrugged. "You've read *Moby Dick.* If our German friend is anything like Captain Ahab, he could have spies in places we can't imagine. We'll not borrow trouble, but we must be cautious."

"The constant suspicion is wearing. I wonder if I'll trust anyone after I get home."

"Perhaps eventually, but it's an occupational hazard, to be sure." He squeezed her arm. "You've not complained once. How is your leg holding up?"

She trembled at his touch. "Achy but manageable. I'm ready to be off my feet, so hopefully we'll find the safe house with no difficulty."

"Agreed." His chuckle was low and warm. "And for the record, pleasure hiking is no longer on my list of hobbies."

She giggled and clapped a hand over her mouth.

They headed toward the tiny hamlet, and she pressed her hand to her chest where her heart bumped in a staccato rhythm. Brave. She must be brave. Her eyes burned as she peered into the inky night, straining to see movement that would indicate they were being watched.

The lane into the village widened, and they crept past the shops, many boarded up. At the second intersection, they turned south and walked to the end of the block. Turning left, they stopped in front of the third stone cottage on the street. A pair of flowerboxes graced the front windows, unfamiliar white blooms nodding in the night air. If a key was under the pile of bushel baskets out back, they were in the right place.

"Wait here." He trotted away.

The hair on the back of her neck prickled, and she whirled. Her gaze bounced from house to house. All was quiet. Was she jumping at shadows, or were their pursuers within striking distance?

Her breath came in ragged bursts, and her vision shimmied. She bent over, and the dizziness passed. She was letting fear get the best of her.

A tiny click sounded, and the door opened in front of her. "All clear." Gerard's whisper penetrated the silence.

She tiptoed inside.

Gerard closed the door and flicked on his flashlight. "Even though the house has blackout curtains, let's leave the lights off until daylight. I'll take first watch. There's a rather decrepit sofa in the living room and a cot in the bedroom. Your choice."

"I'd rather stay in here together, if you don't mind. I'm not sure how much I'll sleep, but getting off this knee sounds heavenly."

He swung the beam around the room until it came to rest on the sofa. "I'll keep guard by the window for now."

Trying not to limp, Emily navigated past two upholstered chairs and a small table surrounded by wooden chairs. A woven rug that had seen better days lay in the center of the room. She dropped onto the end of the couch and sank into the worn cushion. She propped her back against the padded arm and extended her legs. A twinge fluttered through her knee, but the shooting pain had ceased.

The light clicked off, plunging the room in darkness.

She closed her eyes and lowered her chin, willing her muscles to relax and her thoughts to stop racing. Images of the altercation with the Vichy policeman they'd shot replayed through her mind. Her heart sped up, and she blew out a deep breath.

"Emily?"

Her eyes flew open, and she turned her head toward Gerard's voice. "Sorry."

"Nothing to apologize for. Is your knee giving you problems?" Worry covered his words.

"Not as much as I'd thought it would after a trek over hill and dale. No, memories are bubbling up. I can still see the policeman's vacant stare. I've never seen a dead person before. It's...disconcerting."

"Disturbing is more like it, especially with a violent death. We can talk of home to replace the thoughts with something more pleasant. Tell me about your students. Was it hard getting to know them and then lose them at graduation?"

"In some ways, yes. And I shouldn't have favorites, but some kids worked their way into my heart. They were bright, eager to learn, and exhibited such joy when they succeeded. Over the years, a few of them have written letters."

"Their keeping in touch says that you mean a lot to them. You must be a good teacher."

Her face warmed, and she was glad of the darkness so he couldn't see her blush, a habit that was ridiculous at her age. She shrugged. "At twenty-five, I'm not much older, so perhaps they can relate more to me than the older instructors." She giggled. "Many of whom seem old to me."

He snickered. "Your age may be part of it, but I hear the delight in your voice when you talk about them. You love what you do."

"I guess I do. There aren't a lot of employment choices for women, and I fell into teaching, but I enjoy it. And the kids are great."

"Will you visit France after the war? You could bring your students."

"Most don't have the money for foreign travel, and I don't know if the country will be the same for me. My näiveté during my college trip seems so long ago. I'm not the same person."

"None of us are. We—"

Muffled voices sounded.

Emily froze, her stomach roiling. The only people outside at night were the authorities.

"Don't move," Gerard whispered. "We don't want to stumble over furniture and alert them to our presence."

Footfalls thundered on the porch then knocking. "Open up. This is the Vichy police, and we are searching for escaped spies."

Her heart skittered. Should they attempt to leave through the back or take their chances with the cops?

Movement, then Gerard gripped her arm. She jumped at his touch.

He leaned close to her ear, his breath stroking her cheek. "I'd rather not risk another confrontation. Is your leg up for more walking?"

She trembled at his closeness. "It will have to be. Let's go."

"We know you are in there." The harsh tones of the officer's voice filtered through the wooden door.

Pressing her lips together against the pang in her knee, she rolled off the couch, and climbed to her feet. The shadowy outlines of the chairs were visible in the growing light of dawn, and she threaded her way to the door at the rear of the house, Gerard close on her heels.

"We can hope they don't have a guard by the back door."

Gerard's words since a shiver up her spine. She held her breath and turned the knob, praying the hinges wouldn't squeal.

They slipped out of the cottage, and Gerard eased the door closed.

No one greeted them, and Emily heaved a sigh. *Thank You, God.* She trotted to the edge of the property and secreted herself behind a large shrub. Gerald stood close beside her, his body heat warming her arm.

A muted thud sounded from inside the house, then light seeped around the curtains. The police had entered the cottage. How long before they completed their search and went away? Should she and Gerard find somewhere to hide in the hope of being in the area when their contact arrived to lead them to the next destination?

Her palms slicked. The person coming for them needed to be forewarned about the raid. How could they get word to the Resistance? Would the poor soul walk into a trap?

Banging and faint conversation permeated the walls of the cottage.

"Emily, we need to find cover. It's hard to say which direction our pursuers originated from, so we'll have to guess the best place to go."

"Back the way we came, or is that too obvious?"

"Hard to say, but we need to go, now. Dawn is imminent." He jerked his head toward the stone wall that separated the property from the one behind it. "I vote for moving perpendicular to the road rather than alongside it."

"Good idea."

The door to the house swung open, and a figure stood on the threshold. "Our intelligence about an exchange tonight must have been incorrect. Now, we won't get paid. I am not happy."

"Perhaps they have not arrived yet." The second man joined him in the doorway. "We should extinguish the lights and continue to wait. The Nazis give good money for *La Résistance* members."

Her eyes widened, and Gerard's intake of breath was harsh in her ears. The men were not seeking them in particular, but that didn't minimize the danger. Would they never leave? She shifted, and a branch snapped underfoot.

The men's heads swung toward the bush, and one of them shouted, "Someone is out there."

Emily cringed. Had she just condemned Gerard and herself to death?

## Chapter Twenty-Five

Emily gripped Gerard's arm with icy fingers, her heart racing. Her stomach dipped and rolled as nausea threatened to overtake her. She swallowed against the queasiness and prayed she wouldn't lose her last meal. "Should we run?" She pitched her voice low.

"If we move, we'll confirm their suspicions." Close to her ear, he spoke at a whisper.

"Okay."

The policemen unholstered their weapons. Pointing them toward the shrubs, they rushed off the porch then stood at the bottom of the stairs. One of them called out, "Show yourselves, and we will not shoot you."

"Not likely," Gerard mumbled. He squatted and pulled Emily to the ground. "Grab any rocks you can find. On my mark, throw them toward the house on our left. Hopefully, it will make them think we're over there. Then we'll head in the opposite direction."

Her knee protested its bent position, but she pushed aside the ache and felt around the ground, her hands wrapping around several small stones. "Ready."

"Now."

Their ammunition rained down to the ground with muted thuds, and the uniformed men ran toward the sound. Gerard jerked his head in the opposite direction and slipped from behind the shrubbery. Emily held her breath and followed, waiting for the burn of bullets in her back should their pursuers see them fleeing.

They reached the stone wall separating the properties and climbed over the top. One of the boulders shifted, and she fumbled, her ankle twisting. She bit her lip against the pain and dropped to the other side of the barrier.

"Halt!" A shout came from behind them. The policemen hadn't fallen for the ruse and were back on their trail.

Her heart nearly stopped. *Please, God. Keep us safe.*

Gerard hunched over, and she followed suit. Would their low profile be lost amid the shadows despite the growing light? They raced across the backyard of the next house and ducked around the small cottage, then repeated the action until they were several blocks from their original position. Footsteps pounded from behind as their hunters continued to chase them.

A stitch knifed her side, and her lungs were on fire. Each step sent shards of pain through her ankle and knee. Trying not to hobble, she pushed herself to keep up with Gerard whose long legs ate up the distance like a hoard of termites.

They rounded the corner, and he pointed to the spire on the stone church at the end of the street. "There. With any luck, the door will be unlocked, and the priest will give us safe harbor. Or at least stall the coppers for a bit."

Unable to speak, she nodded. They picked up the pace, and her tongue stuck to the roof of her mouth. Seconds later, they reached the front of the chapel. Gerard yanked on the wrought-iron handle, and the scarred wooden doors swung open under his touch.

He cracked a grim smile and gestured for her to precede him.

She stepped into the vestibule, a single candle casting shadows in the gloom. The smell of incense clung to the air. Her ragged breath echoed against the tiles.

Gerard tapped her shoulder. "In here."

They passed into the sanctuary, then froze.

A lone man in a black robe and white collar stood behind the altar. He beckoned them forward, and they hurried up the aisle. "I am Father Remy. You are in need of safe passage, oui?"

Emily gasped. Had God spoken to him like He had the old woman? She claimed to have faith, yet she was stunned each time He provided protection.

"Yes, Father. There are two Vichy policeman who want to turn us in to the occupiers for a bounty." Gerard's forehead wrinkled. "Do you have somewhere we can hide?"

"Come with me. How close are your stalkers?"

"Several blocks, but I'm not sure if they saw us enter your church."

"They will come. The authorities are convinced of my guilt in hiding refugees, but they have yet to find one of them."

"You put yourself in danger for strangers?" Emily's eyes widened.

"As did our Lord. I can do no less." Father Remy shrugged, his face peaceful. "Follow me. We must make haste."

"Merci."

Gerard reached for her hand, and she cradled her palm in his. Warm tingles shot up her arm, and her breath caught. Amazing how safe she felt because of their contact.

The priest led them down a circular sandstone staircase then into a small cell-like room that held a cot, tiny wooden table, and two chairs. A large porcelain vase stood on the floor below an oil painting of a vineyard. "My family's property." He rolled up the rug, exposing a small door. He tugged on the steel ring, and the hatch opened, revealing a dark chasm. "Wait down there. I will come for you when it is safe."

Emily shuddered then followed Gerard down the hole. The lid closed, scraping sounded overhead, then footsteps faded.

He pulled her to him, his heart thumping in a steady bump against hers.

She sighed and melted into his arms. Safety. For now.

Minutes passed.

Clomping, then voices.

"We know they are here. There is nowhere else they could have gone at this hour."

"I don't know what you are talking about. I have been praying through the night."

A slap sounded. "Stop lying. You are known to harbor fugitives and Resistance members."

"I am a simple priest who serves the people of this village."

Another slap. "We will find these renegades, then we will have the proof we need that you are a traitor."

Emily cringed, and silent tears trickled down her cheeks. *Please, God, don't let them kill that man. Surely, he is doing Your will.*

Gerard ran his hands over her hair then stroked her back.

"I'm—"

"Nothing you say will make me believe in your innocence." The sound of a fist striking skin reverberated through the enclosed space. Then another. And another.

Her tears tumbled faster, and Emily bit her lip to keep from crying out. The policeman had apparently decided to try beating the information from Father Remy. How much evil had overtaken these officers that they found satisfaction in attacking a man of God? With each punch, their victim groaned, but he didn't reveal their location.

"Enough! They are not here as this man claims, or he is willing to die to protect them. Either way, we'll get nothing more. Let's go."

"Oui."

"Rest assured, Priest. We will be watching you."

Muffled steps faded. Time crawled.

Finally, a shuffling noise, and then the door opened. Light pierced the enclosure.

Emily squinted against the glare.

"The police are gone. We are safe for the time being." Father Remy spoke through swollen lips.

Emily and Gerard crept from the hiding place and returned the rug and table to their locations.

Her heart tugged. "Father, your face…"

"It is nothing, child. We must get you on your way. But first sustenance for the journey."

"We will get food after I've treated your wounds. I won't take no for an answer, Father."

Gerard chuckled. "It's best to listen to her when she gets like this, Father."

Father Remy snickered then grimaced and nodded.

After cleaning his lacerations, Emily told the priest to remain seated while she and Gerard cooked breakfast. He obeyed without question, and she frowned. He must hurt more than he would have them believe.

Rummaging in the small kitchen, they put together a meal of eggs, cheese, and bread. Father Remy blessed the food, and they ate quickly. When they finished, he rose with a groan and cradled his middle with his arms.

Emily cocked her head. "Do you think your ribs are broken?"

"Non, just bruised."

"How can you be sure?"

"Because they have been broken in the past, and this morning's pain doesn't seem to indicate a fracture."

She started to speak, and he stilled her with a frown. "It is best not to ask too many questions."

"Of course, Father. Forgive me."

"No need for apologies, my child." He jerked his head toward a trunk at the far end of the room. "Inside you will find religious attire. There should be items appropriate for your size. At the bottom, there are civilian items. Take some of those, too. You may have to change along the way."

Emily nibbled her lower lip. "Is it right to impersonate people of the cloth?"

Father Remy sighed. "Despite the malevolence that stalks this land, and the two evil men who were here, priests and nuns generally are not accosted. I am at peace with our actions. Now, put on the items, and I will pack some supplies while you dress."

Gerard followed Father Remy from the room, and Emily donned the coarse, black habit. She tugged the unfamiliar items onto her body. *Please forgive me, Lord, if wearing this garb is offensive to You.* Her new disguise complete, she hurried to the kitchen then stopped short. Uncertainty was etched on Gerard's face above his priestly vestments. He appeared as uncomfortable as she was about their apparel.

"Here." Father Remy held out a bulging satchel. "Bicycles are in the larder. Take them to the next village and leave them at the church. My counterpart will see they are returned. There is a train depot, and the stationmaster is…uh…sympathetic to the cause. There is a tri-color ribbon in your bag. Give it to the man, and he will provide your tickets at no charge. Godspeed. I will pray for your safety."

"Merci, Father. We won't forget your kindness." Gerard pressed several coins into his hand. "It's not much, but I'm sure you'll put it to good use. Perhaps for your next…guests."

Swallowing against the lump in her throat, Emily nodded. "I will pray for you and your work, Father."

"You must hurry. The train leaves in less than two hours."

With a wave, they left the kitchen and retrieved the bikes. Gerard hefted the pack onto his back then mounted his ride, Emily close behind him. The sun peeked over the horizon as they pedaled along the dirt-packed road that led to the next village. Emily's knee protested, but she struggled on. Birds awakened and chirped greetings to the coming day.

Their path intersected then paralleled the railroad tracks, and they followed the line into the picturesque hamlet. Emily shook her head. Pristine views such as this almost made her forget the world was at war. Memories of countryside picnics and hikes with her classmates edged into her mind. Good times. Would peace ever return?

Arriving at the church, they found the priest and gave him the bikes. He seemed unsurprised to see them. "The depot is on the other side of the square at the end of the street. God bless you."

Fifteen minutes later, they crossed the grassy expanse and approached the station. Even with the early hour, the platform was crowded. Mothers soothed crying babies. Young women waited in silence. A trio of old men stood near a stack of luggage, mumbling among themselves.

Emily wiped her damp palms on the scratchy, black fabric. Her eyes darted back and forth looking for policemen...their policemen.

Gerard cleared his throat. "You seem ready to jump out of your skin. You're a nun." His mouth curved in a crooked grin. "Try to look less stressed...more peaceful."

She blew out a breath and forced a smile then stiffened. Beside her, Gerard gasped.

A Mercedes sedan rumbled to a stop, and two SS officers climbed from the vehicle.

## Chapter Twenty-Six

Gerard clenched his jaw. Would they never catch a break? France was crawling with Germans, so he shouldn't be surprised at the SS officers' presence, but one day without the Krauts breathing down his neck would be appreciated. He tugged at his collar then dropped his hands. Fidgeting might draw unwanted attention. He lowered his head and intertwined his fingers in front of him. Should he affect a physical abnormality? A man his age was suspect even when wearing the cleric's clothing.

"We should split up." Emily nudged his shoulder. "I'm not sure about staying in this garb, but if the SS is still looking for us, they are seeking two people. Traveling separately may be our best bet. At least for the next leg or two of the trip."

He pressed his lips together then gestured to a bench behind a pillar. Perhaps they could escape notice being tucked away from the main waiting area. Was dividing up the safer option? His heart constricted. He would not be able to protect Emily if she left his side. Surely, there was another way.

She seated herself then crossed her ankles and folded her hands in her lap. "I can tell by your expression, you're opposed to the suggestion.

Frankly, I'm terrified at the idea of going it alone, but we need to be smart about our travels if we're going to survive."

"And the student becomes the teacher." He smirked. "You're right, of course, but I don't have to like it."

Her face pinked, and a smile tugged at her lips. "The question is whether to remain as clergy or not."

"For the time being, I will keep up the ruse of being a priest. A young man out of uniform is highly irregular, but one of the cloth less so. An acolyte wouldn't be traveling on her own. You should put on the civilian clothing Father Remy gave you. Then we can travel separately on the same train."

"That's a good idea." Her blush deepened. "Although it will be hard to be nonchalant with you in the same car."

"My personality that compelling, is it?"

"Something like that." Emily snickered, then her smile faltered. "The chronic lying is difficult, you know? Not just the remembering part, but our constant subterfuge makes me suspect everyone we interact with."

"That attitude will keep you safe. You're in enemy territory. No one should be trusted. Even those supposedly part of the Resistance or claiming to be an ally. Someone once said that every man has his price. Stories abound about those who have turned in friends, family members, or loved ones."

She shuddered.

He resisted the urge to put his arm around her to comfort her. Physical contact while disguised as they were would surely attract the Nazis' attention. He sighed. They'd been lucky so far. Emily's beauty hadn't caught the Germans' eyes. It didn't matter what he was wearing. Once they got a look at her, he'd become invisible. "Rub some dirt on your face and make your hair unkempt. Even in nun's attire and peroxided hair, you're a lovely-looking woman. Dressed in streetwear, you're sure to cause a ruckus."

"I don't—"

"No, really. You're a looker, so we need to make sure those lads in gray don't notice you." He heard the harshness in his tone and winced. How could she be so unaware of her beauty? Had none of her male classmates asked her out? Were they blind? "I don't mean to embarrass you, but we need to be realistic. Many of the Germans are bullies and need very little excuse to lord their presence over the population. Numerous reports have indicated they also take what they like. We need to make sure you're not on the menu."

Emily ducked her head, her face pale. "Point taken, but we shouldn't be on the same mode of transportation. An observant soldier might think we're together." Her jaw was firm. "If those guys take the next train, I'll get on the one after that. See if you can cycle or hitch a ride to Port-La-Forêt. We'll meet there."

"You'll have to show your papers." He frowned. She was right about needing to travel alone, but he didn't have to like the idea.

"It's a chance we have to take." She squeezed his hand. "I'm not being reckless. God can blind the eyes of our enemy. He has protected us thus far. Let's pray He continues to do so."

Gerard licked his lips. There it was again, her unshakeable faith. Certainty that God would whisk them on their way.

Distant rumbling sounded. The train whistle shrieked. Moments later, the platform vibrated, and the belching iron monster clattered into the station before grinding to a halt. The coal smoke scratched his throat. Passengers clambered on and off. Twenty yards away, the two SS officers climbed into one of the cars.

Emily picked up her satchel. "They're leaving. I'll put on my new guise and wait for the five o'clock train. Go. Find a way to Port-La-Forêt. I'll be fine. Spent time there during my student days. There's a fountain in the middle of the square. Let's meet there at four o'clock in the afternoon. Will that give you enough time to…uh…make arrangements for your travel?"

He checked his watch and pressed his lips together. Not quite twenty-four hours. "Should be enough. As long as I don't run into…complications. The next train will get you there early evening. You'll have to find somewhere to hide out. Could make for a long night."

Her left eye closed in a slow wink. "Your training will do me well, *Major.* I will see you tomorrow afternoon."

"I have no doubt about it, mademoiselle." With a dry mouth, he watched her saunter into the station. Worry nipped his heels, and he hunched his shoulders as he strode from the railroad yard. There was not enough time to proceed on foot, so he would *liberate* a motorized vehicle. Unfortunately, the only folks driving automobiles were farmers, delivery men, and the military. He couldn't take away someone's livelihood, and he wasn't holding the correct papers to use an authorized vehicle. He'd be stopped and arrested before he ever left the village.

Ambling through the streets, he inventoried the battered and broken-down bicycles tucked next to shabby homes. The idea of pedaling the fifty-five miles to their rendezvous held no appeal, walking even less so.

With eyes downcast, an old woman swept the front steps of her home. He had no doubt she watched his every movement. Near the end of the block, a trio of boys squatted over a game of marbles. Farther down, a passel of little girls jumped rope. A petite, brunette youngster with porcelain skin turned toward him, her gap-toothed smile lighting up her face. Intelligence radiated from her hazel eyes.

Emily. Is this what she'd looked like as a child? He blinked and shook away the question. Would she survive the night? He had to believe she would.

The next street over, two women pushed their babies' carriages, ignoring the infants' cries as they laughed and chatted. More houses. More bicycles.

Gerard blew out a deep breath. *Lord, I'm new at trusting You again, and perhaps You're tired of having me only speak to You during times of desperation, but I can really use Your help. Emily and I have been winging it, and so far, and I have a feeling You're a big part of our success. Can I ask You one more time to work a miracle for me? I need some wheels.*

A ball whizzed past his head, and he balked, raising his hands in defense.

"*Je suis désolé, mon père.*" A boy of about ten years old trotted toward him.

He picked up the toy and handed it to the child. "*Ça va.*"

The boy ran back to his friends, and Gerard smiled. Nice to see some normalcy in France. Hopefully, the war would be over before these kids were old enough to be conscripted.

A door opened on the side of the house, and a young woman beckoned to the group. "*À table!*"

Cheering, the children raced toward her. They filed inside, and the door closed with a bang.

Gerard's eyes widened. Nestled in the shadow, a dented motorcycle leaned against the wall. He grinned and refrained from letting out a whoop. *Thank You, Father.* Staring at the vehicle, he nibbled his lower lip, then chuckled to himself. He had picked up Emily's mannerism.

He could pay for the bike, but it would take his funds down to next to nothing. Would the family let him borrow it? With a shrug, he headed for the house. There was only one way to find out. Smoothing his jacket, he raised his hand to knock. Before he could make contact, the door swung open. It was the woman he'd seen earlier stood on the threshold, uncertainty in her eyes.

"Are you hungry, monsieur?"

"Non." He bowed. "I have need of your motorcycle." He fumbled in his pocket. "I can pay you."

"That won't be necessary. You may take it. We no longer have a use for it." A shadow of pain flickered across her face. "It belongs…belonged to my husband."

"*Mes condoléances.*" He gulped. Had the poor woman's mate been marched off to the labor camps or worse? Gerard pressed a fistful of francs into her palm. "*Merci.* God bless you."

"And you." She spoke over her shoulder to someone, and one of the children handed her a towel-wrapped bundle. "Bread for your journey."

"You have many mouths to feed. I can't—"

"It's nothing. May you find success with your task." She glanced down the street. "You must go. The evening patrols being soon. The key is in the ignition, and it is full of *de l'essence.*"

"Again, thank you."

She nodded and closed the door.

*Take care of her, Father.* Gerard climbed onto the bike. He worked through the start-up steps then set the choke into position. Kicking the pedal a few times, he pulled back on the choke and turned the key. The generator light illuminated, and he nearly cheered with relief. He kicked the pedals again and gave the engine some throttle. The machine coughed, roared to life, then stuttered. He pulled back the advancer, and the engine purred. He smiled. Too bad tonight wouldn't be a pleasure ride. With Emily on the back, her supple arms around his waist, touring the French countryside would be a dream come true.

He steered the bike toward the outskirts of the village, and his heart fell.

Parked in the middle of the street, a *Kübelwagen*, the German version of a Jeep, blocked his exit. Two soldiers stood in front of the vehicle, rifles pointed at his chest.

Chapter Twenty-Seven

Emily unclenched her hands and wiped her damp palms on her skirt. She glanced at the other passengers on the train and sighed. Each one seemed lost in his or her own world, studiously avoiding anyone else's eyes. Staring out the window, hidden behind newspapers, pretending to sleep, her fellow travelers sought anonymity and invisibility. The longer the occupation lasted, the more France's citizens developed into frightened and distrustful souls. She shook her head. The lighthearted, cultured country she'd grown to love as a visiting student was being crushed under German boots.

She looked at the empty seat next to her and frowned. Despite the danger, at some level, roving France with Gerard had been exciting and fulfilling. She'd never felt more alive, and his intelligence, sharp wit, and ability to handle any situation that arose intrigued her. He was unlike any man she'd ever met, especially the immature boys of her college years whose goals seemed to revolve around alcohol, drag racing, and playing pranks.

Her mission with Gerard had been a failure. A few messages sent then she'd had to leave the radio behind during the escape. Emily gripped the folds of her skirt, crushing the material. She squeezed her eyes shut then lowered her chin to her chest. They'd been discovered. She sighed. What could she have done to avoid detection?

Across the aisle, a man slid down his window, the muffled chugging of the wheels becoming sharp and clear. A fresh breeze swirled through the car, wiping away the stagnant smell of sweat, coal, and wet wool. Behind her, a toddler fussed, and the soft tones of a woman hushed the child with a word.

Emily rubbed the leather cushion to her right. Had Gerard secured transportation? Would he be at the fountain, his handsome, rugged face wearing a grin when she appeared? Her stomach buzzed as if dozens of squirrels danced the Charleston, and she pressed her hand against her middle. Was her attraction to him merely schoolgirl infatuation or the result of surviving threats of peril and death together for countless days?

She and Gerard had lived a lifetime in a few short months. Experiences she'd never imagined, not in her wildest dreams. No wonder she felt closer to him than anyone she'd ever known. None of her friends and family could understand or relate. After she got home, would she look back on these days with nostalgia or grief?

Scenery through the grimy glass panes blurred like an impressionist painting. Green, gray, and brown melding into a jumble of color. Time marched on, and the cornflower-blue sky darkened to steel, then sapphire, then finally jet black. Her head nodded with the rhythmic clack of the wheels. Did she dare sleep?

The door at the back of the car opened, sending a blast of air into the car. It banged shut, and she jumped. Stifling the urge to see who'd entered, she plucked at the edge of her sleeve.

Heavy footfalls marched toward the front. A muted gasp then murmuring. The baby cried. Apparently, the infant didn't like whomever appeared any more than its fellow passengers. Hairs on the back of Emily's neck prickled. She no longer doubted their newest voyager was either a German soldier or her worst nightmare, an SS agent.

The gray-uniformed figure of an SS officer dropping into the seat next to her confirmed her fears. She slowed her breathing, hoping her heart would follow. This man could extinguish her life with a simple command.

He glanced down his aquiline nose at her, his ice-blue gaze nailing her to the seat. Thin lips were drawn into a slash. Receding straw-colored hair barely covered his scalp, yet his smooth skin was that of a young man. The three diamonds on his shoulder told her he had done well despite his apparent youth. Not a good sign in an organization that seemed to pride itself on cruelty.

She pulled her satchel closer then lowered her eyes. *Please, Lord, keep me safe from this danger.*

"*Guten Abend.*"

Her head raised, and she gave him a demure smile.

He switched to French. "How are you enjoying your journey?"

"Very well. Thank you." Training told her to make him work for the conversation. If she volunteered information, she'd lose control of the situation. If she had any in the first place.

"A lovely night for a train ride, yes?"

"Yes."

"You're not very talkative." He frowned. "Do you fear me?"

"Well…uh…I don't understand why such an important man as yourself would bother with the likes of me. I'm in awe of your presence."

The officer lifted his chin. "It's good you recognize my prominence. Not all of you French do so." He narrowed his eyes. "How do you feel about our presence in your fine country? Life is better, is it not?"

She swallowed. What to say to this odious man? If she was too ingratiating, he might get suspicious of true loyalty. "In some ways, yes."

He threw back his shoulders and guffawed. "An honest woman. How about that?" A smile tugged on the corner of his mouth. "In what ways has your existence not improved?"

"It is difficult to get food sometimes. Many people go hungry."

His face darkened. "Yes, an unfortunate situation. Perhaps if your underground countrymen would not blow up railroad tracks, we could bring food."

"Yes, sir."

"You appear to be traveling alone." He patted her knee, then rested his hand on her leg. "Do you have no family?"

Beneath the fabric of her skirt, her skin crawled. Her hand itched to slap the man. "My husband died, and I am going home to my parents. They are elderly, so it will be good to be together."

He removed his hand from her thigh as if scalded. "You are…were married. How did he die?"

Her heart pounded. The more he quizzed her, the more information she needed to retain. What could she tell him that couldn't be traced but would satisfy his curiosity? Which lie should she promulgate? *God, forgive me.* "A heart attack. We had a small farm, and he was working the fields."

"Was he an old man?"

"No, but the doctor said that perhaps his heart was weak, and we didn't know it."

"If he was a young man, why wasn't he in your armed forces?" The man's expression was inscrutable.

Emily's mind raced. "He was, but after being wounded during the Battle of France, he was mustered out. The shrapnel is…was still in his leg. The military could no longer use him. The factories didn't want him either, so we rented a property and began farming." She pressed her lips together. Hopefully, he'd think her response was grief and not an effort to stem her babbling.

"Do you parents know you're coming?"

"No. I didn't want to worry them about my travel. It will be a surprise. A pleasant one I hope. After all, I'm another mouth to feed. I will try to find work, but…" She shrugged.

"What are your skills?" His eyes narrowed. "The Third Reich offers many opportunities."

Finally, a topic she could speak about without worry. "I am a teacher."

"You work with youngsters."

"Yes, and it is my greatest joy." She chuckled. "My greatest frustration sometimes, also. Do you have any children…I'm sorry, I don't know your rank…?"

"Hauptsturmführer Merkel. Not yet."

"Then you are married."

"Nein." A shadow passed over his face. "I was engaged…once…but she died."

"I'm sorry for your loss."

He waved his hand. "That was a long time ago. Now, I focus on the cause…on ushering in the New Order."

Emily tilted her head. Could she work his grief to her advantage? "You do not look older than me. Surely, your loss wasn't too far in the past. Would it help to tell me about her?"

Uncertainty flickered in his eyes, then they shuttered. "I will be the one to ask questions. This conversation is not about me, no matter how much you try to change the topic, Frau...?" His left eyebrow raised. "You know my name. Won't you share yours?"

Her palms slicked. Would he then ask for her papers? For proof? Why had she ever thought riding the train would allow her to escape unnoticed? She forced a smile. "Frau Suard. I apologize for my ill manners. I should have introduced myself when you sat down. My parents would not be happy at my gauche behavior, but I was disquieted by your presence."

"Of course you were." He rubbed his jaw. "Are you any relation to Amélie Suard, the writer from the French Revolution?"

She chilled. "You certainly know your French history." What else did he know? "Where did you get such remarkable knowledge?"

The door banged open at the far end of the car. "Tickets. Papers and tickets, please."

Emily's mouth lost all moisture, and her tongue stuck to the roof of her mouth.

Hauptsturmführer Merkel lifted his chin. "Part of my officers training was to study past wars and uprisings. Because I was a selected for France, I did a bit of extracurricular reading."

He touted his keen mind and prodigious memory, but Emily turned one ear toward the approaching footsteps of the porter. She was trapped between the window and the German with no chance of escape. The odds of breaking past Merkel were poor. Too low to overcome? She relived her training that taught her how to *neutralize* an opponent.

Emily's fingers flexed. The muscles in her legs tightened. Surprise would be key. Beating like a tympani, her heart threatened to jump from her chest. Seconds passed in slow motion as the ticket taker made his way along the aisle, one slow step at a time.

Three rows behind her…then…two…one.

The lanky, gray-haired porter arrived at their seats. His gaze flickered from Merkel to her, poorly masked revulsion flooding his expression. He obviously thought she was with the SS officer, but would soon discover his error.

He bowed slightly. "Tickets and papers, please."

Merkel waved his hand in dismissal.

Eyes widening, the porter blanched. "Sir, I'm afraid I must ask you again." He stuttered. "The railway line could get in trouble for not following protocols. It is a requirement of the Reich to review identity cards along with tickets."

"And I can override formalities, can't I? Now, move along, man, or I'll have you arrested."

Why would Merkel refuse to show his tickets? Was God going to use her enemy to protect her? *You never cease to amaze me, Lord.*

Nodding, the porter stumbled forward and snatched the papers from the extended hand of an elderly woman in front of her.

"Well, that was a close one, wasn't it?" Merkel's voice held sarcasm, and his eyes glinted as they pinned her against the seat.

## Chapter Twenty-Eight

Gerard low and gunned the motorcycle engine. In a burst of speed, the vehicle shot forward. He zigzagged down the road, his wheels spitting grit and rubble. The rearview mirror registered dust clouds.

Gunfire crackled.

Bullets whizzed past him. One pinged off the side of the bike. He flinched then downshifted and careened around the roadblock with inches to spare. His heart pounded as if he were running a race. Perspiration broke out on his forehead and trickled down his spine.

He roared ahead, the barrage fading as the bike ate up the miles. His ears strained for the sound of trucks, but no rumbling followed him. Either the soldiers decided he wasn't worth the effort or they radioed the next village to be on the lookout for him. Reason enough to eventually get off the road, with or without the bike.

Deep breaths cleared the adrenaline from his system, but his mind continued to ruminate over the situation. Had Emily evaded the SS officers? Or had her beauty drawn their scrutiny? She'd proven her abilities and her toughness, but the cruelty of Hitler's elite was legendary. Even the staunchest agents sometimes gave way under their torture.

"Please, God, keep her safe."

Bouncing over the uneven macadam, Gerard searched the countryside as he rode. Dips and bumps jostled the bike. He tightened his grip on the handlebars, his sweat-slicked palms struggling to maintain a hold.

In a field to his right, several emaciated cows poked their noses toward the ground nibbling at the sparse, brown grass. The herd, if he could call it that, lifted their heads as one and watched him pass. In front of a distant barn, the tiny figure of a man also seemed to observe his progress. He lifted his arm in acknowledgment but received no return wave. The farmer was probably suspicious of anyone on a motorized vehicle. After all, who could afford or acquire the fuel?

He continued on for another hour, then two. His body ached from straddling the cantankerous machine.

A signpost appeared. Fifteen more kilometers to the village. How close should he approach before ditching the bike?

As if responding to the unspoken question, the motorcycle coughed and sputtered. More coughing and a bang, then nothing. Gerard glanced at the gas gauge and sighed. He was out of petrol. Apparently, he was done with the bike and needed to get it off the road. He'd stash the motorcycle in the woods.

With dusk approaching, he had to hurry to make it to the tiny hamlet before curfew. Or should he hide out in the forest for the remainder of the night and most of tomorrow in order to arrive only a short time before the rendezvous? He rubbed his stiff fingers over his face. Since when was he so uncertain with his choices? If anything, he was usually accused of making unilateral decisions and sorting out the consequences afterward.

Another sigh escaped. He knew exactly why he was second-guessing himself, and her name was Emily. He finally understood what the military had been trying to drill into him. Every action has reaction, and that repercussion impacts platoon mates, and in this case, a partner. He couldn't be the reason she was compromised or captured.

Gerard thrust the machine through the trees then dragged it deeper into the foliage. With a grunt, he yanked it over boulders and depressions in the terrain, the scent of evergreen trees melding with the earthy aroma of the soil. Overhead, squirrels scolded his invasion of their territory.

About a hundred yards from the road, he stopped and hid the bike under a large shrub he didn't recognize. Not that his knowledge of France's flora would win any awards. He walked around the bush and checked his handiwork from all angles. Satisfied the bike was concealed from prying eyes, he surveyed the surrounding area. Now to find somewhere to get some sleep.

The sound of an engine came from the direction of the road. Then doors closing and voices. His heart jumped to his throat. Had soldiers from the blockade tracked him? More likely, it was a search party from his destination. Either way, he had to find somewhere to hide. Quickly. He swiveled his neck and studied the landscape. Lots of pine and spruce. If he climbed high enough, perhaps the enemy wouldn't see him.

He picked his way over the undulating terrain, mindful of fallen branches that would give away his position if he stepped on them. A larch stood between two pines, its limbs thick and sturdy looking

Perfect.

Voices wafted toward him on the breeze, but he was unable to make out the guttural words, signifying the men were Germans. His chest tightened. It was now or never.

He grasped the lowest branch and began to climb, ascending the tree until he was twenty feet above the forest floor. He pressed his back flush to the trunk with one arm at his side, and the other angled as if it belonged to the larch. Forcing himself to slow his breathing, he froze in position.

Footsteps came closer, the conversation louder. He nearly laughed when he translated their words. They complained about the order to search the woods. This stop was their fourth, and the men were cranky about their lack of success, but especially about being pulled away from their meal.

From the noise they made, their search was half-hearted at best. More griping, then they agreed there was no one was hiding in the forest. They marched off, and moments later, their vehicle roared to life and rumbled away.

Another narrow escape. *Thank You, Lord.*

The Germans' appearance clinched his decision. He would remain in the woods for the night and set off for the village after the sun was somewhat high in the sky, so he wouldn't have to kill time in a location where soldiers were looking for him. Would Emily be at the fountain?

———————————

Brakes squealed, and wisps of smoke belched past the window next to Emily as the train lurched to stop at the Port-la-Forêt station. Her stomach clenched. The last two hours had consisted of veiled comments by Hauptsturmführer Merkel followed by his travelogue of history and culture about the area, all delivered with a perfect French accent.

The SS officer seemed to enjoy toying with her. He'd been gracious and polite, but underneath his manners brewed darkness. He rose and offered her his arm.

She hesitated and nibbled her lower lip. Was he escorting her to freedom or shackles?

"Please, let me help you, Frau Suard. The journey has been arduous. You must be stiff from sitting so long." He leaned close. "No need for you to deal with the hassle of security."

With a shrug, Emily tucked her hand in the crook of his elbow and slung her satchel over her shoulder. They made their way off the train into the dimness of the evening. A few stars peeked through the deepening night sky. A fingernail-shaped moon hung low. The smell of coal, grease, and creosote permeated the cool air, and the conductor shouted commands over the murmur of conversation from the crowd.

Her hand gripping the rough fabric of his sleeve, she hurried to keep pace with his long strides. They entered the tiny stone hut that served as the station. Near the ticket window, three hulking, black-coated SS soldiers glowered in their direction, bringing to mind smuggled photos she'd seen from the Berlin victory parade after the fall of France. Apparently, these men hadn't received word about Himmler's recall of the uniforms in favor of the gray-green design Merkel wore. She shuddered. The black uniforms seemed more frightening.

One by one, passengers stopped in front of one of the soldiers to show their identity cards and tickets. The men pored over each document then motioned the traveler forward.

With a wave, Merkel circumvented the queue and headed for the exit, Emily still on his arm.

The stockiest of the soldiers, reminiscent of the mastiff who lived next door to Emily's family back home, stepped forward. "Hauptsturmführer, we need to process your…uh…companion."

A chill swept over Emily.

Merkel frowned. "Nonsense. There is nothing you need to know about this woman save that she is with me, thereby giving her all the authorization she needs to visit this village. Concern yourself with the others."

"Sir, I'll have to report this incident."

Raising to his full height, Merkel marched to the man, dragging Emily with him. He looked down his nose, his eyes slivers of blue ice. "With my rank being far above yours, I do not answer to you. There is no incident. Therefore, there is nothing to report. You've obviously been assigned to this puny, insignificant outpost for your incompetence. Don't exacerbate your situation by questioning my actions. I've a mind to have you sent to the Eastern Front."

The soldier seemed to shrink before Emily's eyes. "That won't be necessary, sir. My apologies for being overzealous with my task."

Merkel sniffed. "Don't let it happen again." He turned on his heel and stalked to the exit.

"Yes, sir." The man's mumbled response barely met Emily's ear.

Would she be subjected to Merkel's withering anger? Was he truly protecting her, or did he prefer to handle her torture himself? She stumbled at the thought.

Her companion stopped. "Are you all right? Forgive my haste."

"I'm fine. Just fatigued. As you said, it was a difficult journey. I'm just now getting feeling back in my legs."

He nodded. "I will escort to your parent's home. It is apparent by that *dummkopf's* actions, you may not be safe alone."

"There is no need. I will be stopping by the market, so I don't arrive empty handed. And it might be awkward if I show up on the arm of an SS officer." Her shoulders stiffened. Would she never rid herself of this man? Why didn't he arrest her and get the torment over with? His solicitous behavior was nerve wracking.

A long moment passed as he studied her face.

She held his gaze, praying he would see no subterfuge.

He sighed then withdrew a card from his breast pocket. "If you experience any trouble at all, use this, and I will come to your aid."

The thick ivory card was embossed with his name and rank. She frowned. What German soldier carried a calling card? She tucked it into her satchel. "Thank you. I appreciate all you've done for me, but I don't understand why."

A soft smile tugged at the corner of his mouth. "Not everyone is as they seem, Frau Suard. Thank you for helping pass the time with this war-weary soldier."

She stifled the urge to curtsy. Instead, she extended her arm.

His warm, calloused palm enveloped hers. He clicked his heels and bowed over their clasped hands. "Godspeed."

Her eyebrows shot up, but she managed to stutter, "And to you as well."

Without another word, he released her fingers and strode away, his tall figure soon swallowed up in the throng of people leaving the station.

Her heart jackhammered in her chest. Her breath ragged, she leaned against the square, yellow mailbox nearby. The cold metal seeped through her clothes, breaking her reverie. *Thank You, God.* She searched the sky for a spire that would indicate the village church and smiled. Spending the night on a hard pew might not be a comfortable choice, but if God continued to protect her as He had, the bench was her safest choice. Where was Gerard sleeping tonight?

## Chapter Twenty-Nine

Rainbows of light flitted across the pew and into Emily's half-open eyes. She squinted against the glare and groaned. Her muscles ached, protesting as she sat up on the hard wooden bench. The priest had not asked any questions, but instead prayed with her, then provided a small meal of bread and cheese before handing her a blanket. She rubbed her shoulder and fingered the scratchy wool. She didn't want to look a gift horse in the mouth, but she'd give a month's salary, maybe more, for one of her mother's soft crocheted afghans.

She sat up and glanced at her watch. Last night's exhaustion had caused her to sleep longer than expected. Only a few minutes remained before she could head to the fountain to meet Gerard. Her heart skittered, and her face warmed. Less than a day since she'd seen him, yet it felt like a week. She shook her head. Focus, Emily.

Her stomach gurgled. She'd stop by the market on the way to pick up something to eat. And enough for Gerard in case he hadn't received hospitality as she had.

Footsteps shuffled across the stone floor. The elderly priest smiled as he approached. "I hope you slept well, mademoiselle."

"Oui. Thank you for allowing me to stay. Are you sure I haven't put you in danger?"

The man shrugged. "Only God knows, but until He tells me differently, I will shelter His children and provide sustenance." He held out an apple and hunk of bread. "You must be tired of eating bread, but I'm afraid I haven't much else to offer."

"Merci. You are generous to share from what little you have."

"I assume you will be moving on today."

"Yes." She dug into her pocket then pressed several coins into the priest's hand. "Please use this to further your mission. I will pray for your safety."

"Bless you, child." He patted her arm then tilted his head. "You are meeting someone special? Underneath your fatigue and wariness, I see excitement and anticipation."

Her face warmed, and she ducked her head. "I cannot—"

He chuckled. "There is no need for explanations, child. I'm glad you have found happiness in these dark times." He made the sign of the cross over her then toddled away, his shoes scraping against the bare floor.

Emily bowed her head. "Thank You, God, for this man who has answered Your call to serve. Please keep him safe. Help me be as brave in the face of possible death. Please let Gerard be at the fountain, and lead us across the border without further incident."

She looked up. Above her head, the stained-glass picture portraying Jesus and the little children shone in the rising sun. A warm shawl of peace settled over her. Whatever happened, God was in control.

With a nod to herself, she finger-combed her short tresses, then picked up her satchel and hefted it onto her shoulder. She pulled on the heavy wooden door and left the coolness of the sanctuary.

Puffy, white clouds scudded across the sky, and birdsong filled the trees. A soft breeze caressed her cheeks and lifted her hair. She raised her face to the sunlight, smiling as it heated her skin. For a moment, it was easy to forget there was a war raging.

She skirted two women pushing prams, nodding at them as they passed. Hunched over his cane, a gray-haired man hobbled along the sidewalk. A group of children gathered at the entrance to the square.

Emily checked her watch. Right on time. Her gaze bouncing from booth to booth in the market, she searched for Gerard's familiar form. A minute ticked past. Then two. Then ten.

He was nowhere to be seen.

Her heart fell, and she trudged to the limestone fountain. Standing at least eight feet high, the column section was shaped like an urn. Three brass spigots dribbled water into the six-foot-round basin that featured fish carvings. She dabbled her fingers into the cool liquid then dropped onto the edge of the pool. Lips trembling, she lowered her face, and blinked back tears.

"Why so forlorn?"

Her head shot up.

Gerard towered over her, a brazen grin quirking his mouth.

She leapt to her feet and wrapped her arms around him. "You're here!"

His arms encircled her, and he held her close. His heartbeat strong and steady in her ear. His kissed the top of her head and stroked her back, his fingers drawing lazy patterns along her spine.

Her skin tingled at the warmth of his touch.

"Ah, *jeune amour.*" A middle-aged woman chuckled nearby.

Face heating, she pulled back. "I…uh…I'm so glad you're okay."

He tucked his index finger under her chin and lifted until her eyes met his. Still smiling, he nodded, his robin's-egg-blue eyes sparkling. "I would hope so with that kind of greeting. I'm relieved to see you survived your journey as well. You must have lots to tell me about how you evaded the Germans.

"It was hair-raising, but God protected me, and He used an SS officer to do it."

Eyes wide, he cocked his head. "Well, how about that? Listen, I'm famished. Let's grab some food from one of the merchants and head out. I was able to make contact with a local cell and convinced them we're legit. We're to meet one of their operatives at Pontarlier."

"That's a two-day walk."

"Now you know why I want to secure some food." He laughed and ruffled her hair. "Let's snap to it, recruit."

A quick punch to his arm, then giggles, and she retrieved her bag. She slung the satchel over her shoulder as she swaggered toward the booths.

Gerard's rumbling snigger was music to her ears. In two strides, he was at her side. In a fluid motion, he grabbed her hand, placed it on his shoulder, then put his other hand at her waist and waltzed her down the pavement. Humming Waldteufel's "Les Lointains" in a warm baritone voice, he was an adept dance partner.

"Are you trying to call attention to us?" She extricated her hand then wrapped her arms around her middle.

Disappointment washed over his face. He bowed from the waist. "Forgive me, madame. I was caught up in the moment." He wheeled away and continued toward the food vendors.

She sighed. Why did she manage to ruin every good moment they had? Her feet slapped the pavement as she hurried to catch up with him. "Wait, chéri. Forgive me. I'm too serious. I didn't mean to—"

He whirled toward her, his expression shuttered. "There is nothing to forgive. You're right, of course. There were no Germans in sight, and I allowed my feelings of relief and happiness to jeopardize our cover." He huffed out a loud breath. "I'll be glad when we're out of this godforsaken country."

---

Gerard glanced at Emily, who trekked beside him, mouth pressed in a thin line as it had been for most of the last thirty-six hours. No matter how many times he'd apologized for being a boor, Emily hadn't responded with more than a cursory "that's fine." He'd lost count of the number of times she used the phrase which was actually female code for "life is anything but okay."

They'd made good time, covering nearly two-thirds of the distance the first day. A small, abandoned shack provided shelter the previous night, and they'd both slept like the dead. Every muscle in his body ached. She had to feel the same, yet never complained. The sun peaked in the sky a couple of hours ago and now headed toward the horizon, creating long shadows behind them.

A dilapidated wooden sign leaned away from the road as if exhausted. They drew close, and he peered at the faded lettering. Finally, their destination. Now, to wait for their contact.

He unscrewed the lid to the hip flask he'd secured and held it toward Emily. "Water?"

She shook her head.

"You haven't had anything to drink since we started out this morning. You'll get dehydrated. Please, at least take a swig or two."

A shrug. Then she reached for the vessel and tipped it to her lips. She handed it back then wiped her mouth with her sleeve.

The crumbling remains of a stone wall lined the grassy meadow, and he tromped toward the embankment. He lowered himself onto a large, flat boulder and stretched out his legs. He gestured to the rock beside him. "It could be a while before our guide arrives."

Another shrug. She ambled toward the wall and sat down.

He threw up his hands. "Can you stop giving me the silent treatment? I don't know what else to do besides all the apologizing I've already done."

Emily sighed. "It's not you. The problem is me. I'm the one who should be asking forgiveness. I'm grateful to you for giving me this chance, and especially for God's protection in response to all my errors. I should never have come. It's my fault we were compromised."

"No, it's not." He leaned forward to look into her eyes. "Is that what's been eating you these last two days? It's no one's fault. The Germans are formidable opponents, and they found us fair and square. Please, stopping beating yourself up over our situation." His heart tugged. Such an intelligent, tenacious, and beautiful woman to be riddled with insecurities and doubt. "I admit I was dubious about your presence on this mission, but you've performed admirably, and there's no one else I'd rather be working with than you." He pressed his lips together before he blurted out he wanted to be with her, period. Not just for the mission.

"Thanks, that's nice of you to say." She huffed out a breath. "I'm just a bundle of uncertainty, aren't I?"

He grabbed her hand and squeezed it. Her palm fit perfectly within his. "Hey, first assignments are scary, no matter what, but to be behind enemy lines and running for your life...well, that's even more frightening. You begin to second-guess yourself because every decision matters. You are doing great, and we will survive this."

Movement occurred to his right. Two men emerged from the woods about a hundred yards away. He stiffened. His intel said nothing about a second guide. He rose and brushed the dirt off his pants. "Let me take the lead, okay?"

Emily nodded, her posture rigid. "But I'm ready to make a run for it, if necessary."

"Good girl."

She flushed then thrust her shoulders back.

The men approached at a leisurely pace as if out for a Sunday stroll. They brought to mind Mutt and Jeff, one of them tall and lanky, the other short and stocky. The taller of the two was a poster child for Hitler's Aryan ideology, with his white-blond hair that shone even in the fading sunlight. Their clothes were clean but worn, their boots scuffed.

As they got closer, he smiled. The stocky man was OSS. He'd been at the training facility when Gerard had arrived. He searched his memory for the man's name.

Beside him, Emily gasped. She apparently recognized the man, too.

He glanced at her. She wasn't looking at their fellow agent but rather stared at the blond as if facing a ghost. How did she know the man?

"Emily?"

"That's the guy from the train." She barely moved her lips as she spoke. "The SS officer who helped me."

Gerard froze. Was the man Resistance or Nazi trying to infiltrate the Underground? The next few minutes would be very telling.

## Chapter Thirty

Hummingbirds took flight in Emily's stomach. Was Merkel-if that was his name-truly on their side or trying to make them believe in his loyalty to their cause?

"I'd ask if you were sure about this man's identity, but from the look on your face, that would be a foolish question." Gerard stuffed his hands into his front pockets. "Let him indicate if he recognizes you. Otherwise, I'll see what I can find out from the other guide. Do you remember him from the training facility? You may not have run across him during your stay."

Her gaze shot to the other traveler. She narrowed her eyes. His hair was different, shoulder length now, and the goatee softened the angle of his chin, but if she wasn't mistaken, he was one of the instructors she'd not been subjected to. "If you hadn't said anything, I might not have noticed. I'm definitely interested in what he has to say about Merkel, or whatever name he's going to use with us."

The pair drew close.

Emily pinned what she hoped was a nonchalant expression on her face. "Bonne journée." Her toes curled. Would she have the stamina to run if necessary?

"Bonjour." Merkel's eyes widened, and he grinned. He took Emily's hand and bowed. "We meet again, madame. I told you not everyone is as they seem. Apparently, that is true for you as well. Is this your so-called dead husband?"

"I—"

"What is your game?" Gerard whipped out his pistol and pointed it at the man. "She says you're a German, an SS officer."

Merkel released Emily's hand and raised his arms. "I am the product of a mixed marriage. My mother is French, and my father is German, therefore I speak both languages like a native, which means I'm of great use to the Resistance. I managed to penetrate the *Schutzstaffel*. It took months for them to accept me. But now I use my SS connections to travel unrestricted and gain access to important information."

Emily searched his face. His eyes were clear, his expression smooth. She wanted to believe him. "Is your name really Merkel?"

"Oui. But while out of uniform, I am referred to as Caron, my mother's surname."

"Do the Germans know of your French heritage? That would put you under suspicion."

"Fortunately, my mère comes from Vichy, which seemed to count for something. I love Germany, but she can be a great nation without overrunning all of Europe and exterminating ethnic groups."

"Where were you raised?" Gerard stood ramrod straight, revolver still pointed at Merkel.

"We spent six months of each year in Berlin, and the other half of the year in Vichy. My parents were killed during what has been called the Night of Broken Glass."

Emily gasped. *"Kristallnacht."* The incident sent shock waves around the world when it came out in the newspapers. Two long days of terror rained down upon Jews throughout Germany. Synagogues torched, windows smashed, homes and shops vandalized, and Jews murdered while authorities turned a blind eye to the atrocities. "You're Jewish or at least partially. Surely, the Germans would have ferreted out that information."

"There's something you're not telling us." Gerard's voice was hard.

The OSS officer moved between Merkel and Gerard. "Enough. He has been vetted through the Home Office. That is all you need to know. Now, put away your weapon, and let's get moving before we lose more daylight."

Emily swallowed, her eyes darting from man to man. Who would give way first?

"I outrank you, so I suggest you do as you're told. You may call me *Lynx.*"

"The bobcat, eh? Clever." Gerard tucked the pistol in his back waistband. "You may call me *Renard.*"

"The fox?" Lynx shrugged and glanced at the sky. "We'll walk until dark then hole up for the night. I will leave you at Mouthe, and Merkel will guide you over the border into Switzerland."

The muscle in Gerard's cheek jumped, and he gestured for the men to take the lead.

Her breath hitched. She'd been with him long enough to recognize that he was making a show of acquiescence, but watched them like the fox he claimed to be.

---

Emily opened her eyes and sat up. She stretched in an effort to ease the kinks in her body from lying on the hard ground. The men were already up and moving around. She scrambled to her feet, caught Gerard's eye, and jerked her head toward the deep forest.

He nodded and mouthed, "Not too far."

There were many things she would never tell her mother, one of which was spending the night with three men in the woods. She clomped to a thick clump of bushes. Would society ever know about the many women who broke protocols and customs in their effort to save a world at war? She shook her head to clear her thoughts. Much too philosophical this early in the morning.

Moments later, she returned to camp, if that's what it could be called. Gerard tossed her a hunk of bread, and she tore off a piece with her teeth. She tucked the rest of the lump in her pocket, rolled up her blanket, and stuffed it in her pack. Pulling out her brush, she unsnarled the knots in her greasy hair, and grimaced. Oh, for the day when she would be fully clean again. Would she have any chance of dipping in a river sometime soon?

She slid her arms through the straps on her satchel and swung it onto her back. "Ready when you are, gentlemen."

As one, they nodded, donned their packs, then began to tromp up the incline through the trees.

Three hours later, they arrived at Mouthe, and Lynx stopped. "This is where I break off, and you will continue on through the Grand Risoux forest which is a little over twelve square kilometers. From here you must be extra vigilant. The Nazis patrol the border day and night. Anyone found within two kilometers is shot on sight."

Emily performed the conversion of kilometers to miles and sighed. Just over seven miles. The end was in sight, albeit nearly eight treacherous, enemy-filled miles. A border between France and Switzerland, the small three-foot-high drystone wall decorated with fleur-de-lis separated the two countries. The Germans were wise to guard the area.

Gerard and Lynx shook hands. Emily waved her hand. "Godspeed. Thank you for your help."

Lynx returned her farewell then clapped Merkel on the shoulder. "Keep them safe, my friend. I will come back to find you if anything happens to them."

Merkel touched two fingers to his head in a salute. "I have not lost a *réfugié* yet."

"See that this isn't the first time." Lynx turned on his heel and disappeared among the trees.

"He worries too much."

Gerard glared at Merkel. "Perhaps you don't worry enough."

"I understand your distrust, but without me, you would wander through the forest like Hansel and Gretel. I know the best route, and because of my countrymen's preference for strict adherence to schedule, I know when there will be a gap in coverage. We will slip past their detection, and they will be none the wiser."

Emily looked skyward. Is this from You, Father?

*Be strong and of good courage, fear not, nor be afraid of them, the Lord thy God, He that doth go with thee; He will not fail thee nor forsake thee.*

Warmth settled over her. *Thank you, God.* She put her hand on Gerard's arm. "I have peace about this. Let's step out in faith."

His gaze pierced her face for a long moment, his baby blues shards of ice.

She didn't break eye contact, trying to convey her belief that God was going to protect them to the end of the journey.

Merkel waited, arms crossed.

Gerard's lips curved into an imperceptible smile. "Once again, your strength of conviction is greater than my own."

"Your problem, *Major*, is the confidence you place in yourself rather than others." She smiled to take the sting from her words. "And at times that works out for the best, but in this case we need a miracle, and God is in the miracle business."

"Amen." Merkel approached. "He has saved my skin more than once."

Emily's eyes narrowed. "You—"

"Oui, I am a believer in the one true God and His son, Jesus." He cleared his throat. "Now, we must get started if we are to arrive at the precise time needed to scale the wall."

Gerard extended his hand. "Forgive me, brother. I am not one who trusts easily." He grinned. "But I did know you were omitting personal details."

Merkel chuckled. "Indeed."

In the distance, voices filtered through the trees.

Tilting his head Merkel flung his hand to the east. "That way," he hissed. "There is a set of caves approximately fifty meters from here."

They hurried through the woods on the balls of their feet, careful to step over fallen branches that might crackle when broken.

Mouth dry and heart pounding, Emily kept an ear turned toward the voices that seemed to be getting louder. One minute peace, the next sheer terror. Please, God, hide us. And help my unbelief.

Limestone boulders appeared, and Merkel led them to the smallest then gestured to a dark slit barely visible. He slipped inside, and she and Gerard followed on his heels. Dampness enveloped them, the earthy scent of mud and decaying vegetation clinging to the air.

Shaking, she huddled next to Gerard, and he wrapped his arm around her shoulder, his body heat permeating her jacket. She nestled closer, and he stroked her back. He bent and kissed her head, and she smiled in the dim light.

Outside the cave, footsteps plunged through foliage, limbs snapping like gunfire. The men argued among themselves and marched past the rock formations without stopping. Their voices faded, and five minutes later silence reigned in the forest.

Nearby, Merkel let out a loud breath. "A close one, oui?"

"Without a doubt." Gerard's chest vibrated against her side when he spoke.

"Come. Their appearance put us further behind. We must make haste." He leaned toward Emily. "You seem to be more than coworkers, perhaps even more than friends. Be careful."

Emily's gaze shot toward him, but he'd already moved away.

They exited the cave and ascended the mountain, picking their way around shrubs, trees, rocks, and uneven terrain. Their elevation increased, and the temperature dropped. Puffs of steam came from their mouths as they breathed.

Emily rubbed her arms and stuffed her hands into her pockets to warm her fingers. Her toes tingled with cold. She stamped her feet in an effort to keep feeling in them. "How much farther?"

Merkel smiled, his eyes kind. "Getting tired, *mon partenaire?*"

"No, I'm freezing. The hike is keeping me somewhat toasty, but I'd give just about anything for a pair of wool socks and a hat."

"Not far until we turn off to make our approach from the correct side. Then we must maintain strict silence for the last two kilometers until we have traversed the wall. I will motion as appropriate. Watch me, and do exactly as I indicate."

They hiked farther up the mountain, and Merkel gestured for them to walk along the crest. They ducked behind bushes and boulders as they traveled. Hearing the guttural tones of a German patrol, they climbed high in the tree branches until the men disappeared from view.

Heart still hammering, Emily descended the tree and sighed when her soles hit solid ground. They continued on their way for another thirty minutes. Merkel stopped and held up his hand. He pointed through the leaves.

Barely visible, the drystone wall stood as the last barrier to freedom. Tears sprang to Emily's eyes, and she blinked them away. The men would think her ridiculous, a sniveling female. She glanced at Gerard, and a lump formed in her throat. A sheen of moisture covered his eyes. He, too, was overcome with emotion.

A pair of gray-coated soldiers paced in front of the wall, rifles against their shoulders. A few minutes later, one of the men checked his watch then said something to his companion who nodded. They marched away, leaving the area unattended.

Merkel held his forefinger and thumb an inch apart, indicating thirty seconds, then pointed at the barricade.

Gerard stared at his watch as if it were a lifeline. Time ticked forward. "Now." He captured Emily's hand in his and guided her through the shrubbery. Her back sizzled waiting for the hail of bullets should they be discovered. She held her breath as they made their way to the wall.

Closer. Closer.

She pivoted her head back and forth watching for uniforms, her ears straining for the sounds of voices, footsteps, or worse, rifles cocking.

Nothing.

They reached the wall.

Emily glanced at Merkel who gave her an American thumbs-up. How did he know about that? The man was an enigma.

She hesitated.

Gerard pushed her toward the stone. "No time for goodbyes."

Swinging her leg up on top of the wall, she pulled herself over and dropped to the other side. Gerard fell to the earth beside her.

"*Halt!* You there. Put up your hands."

## Chapter Thirty-One

Gerard shielded Emily's body with his own and cupped a hand over her mouth to keep her from crying out. Her gaze ricocheted back and forth from his face to the wall. Heart battering his chest, he looked over his shoulder expecting to see the muzzle of a rifle pointed at them, but nothing appeared over the stone edifice.

"*Herren,* no need to be alarmed." Merkel's voice wafted toward them. "I am Hauptsturmführer Merkel with the SS checking on the security of this post. You have done well by discovering my whereabouts, and your excellent skills will be highlighted in my report."

"SS? Why are you not in uniform? We could have shot you in error." The high-pitched, nasal tones of one of the soldiers sounded derisive. "Where is your identity card?"

"Do not shoot. I'm going to reach into my pocket to retrieve my identification card."

"Make it snappy."

Silence then rustling footsteps.

"Everything appears to be in order, sir." The soldier's voice held respect and fear. "Be careful out there. We could have shot you on sight."

"Understood, but I am following orders by traveling undercover. Sometimes one must give his life for der führer, no questions asked."

"Jawohl, Hauptsturmführer."

"Carry on, Herren.*"

Footfalls faded, and all was quiet. Gerard pulled himself to his knees then climbed to his feet. He peeked over the wall, and the tightness in his chest eased. The soldiers were gone. He motioned to Emily, and she rose, face still ashen.

Gerard pulled her into a quick embrace and kissed her forehead. "We're safe now, but I have no intention of registering with the Swiss authorities and remaining in one of their internment camps. Let's find one of the two huts Merkel mentioned and rest for the night, then make our way to Bern where the OSS has an office. We will report in, and with any luck, they'll send us back to England. I can't imagine they'll keep us in Switzerland, but I gave up guessing what the higher-ups will do a long time ago."

In his arms, her trembling ceased, and she wilted against him. "Rest sounds heavenly. My knowledge of Switzerland is minimal. Is the journey far?"

"Far enough." He didn't have the heart to tell her about the additional ninety miles in their future. However, God had provided thus far. Would He have mercy and send a motorized vehicle?

Following the directions Merkel had outlined, they walked deep into the forest. Squirrels flitted overhead, and chipmunks skittered among the bushes. Chirping and birdcalls filled the trees. It seemed as if even the wildlife celebrated the freedom of living in neutral Switzerland rather than under the oppressive occupation in France.

A wooden shack appeared nestled in a small clearing. Gerard held up his hand. "Let me check out the hut." He pitched his voice low. "It should be empty, but…"

Mute, she nodded and swayed on her feet.

He squeezed her shoulder. "I won't be long. Grab on to one of the trees for support."

She sighed and leaned against the wide trunk of an oak.

On the balls of his feet, he crept forward and pressed his ear against the side of the building. Nothing. He walked around the corner and repeated the action. Still no noise from inside. A tiny window was in the middle of the next wall, and he crouched below the glass, ears straining for sound.

Still nothing. He slowly raised himself above the sill and peeked through the grimy panes.

Vacant.

He smiled and hurried to Emily's location. "We can enter. The wooden chairs and cots might not be too comfortable, but at least we'll be out of the elements."

She rubbed her hands together, relief smoothing her features. "Sounds good to me."

They entered the hut, and Gerard gaped at the provisions. A small basket held canned food, and a larger basket was piled with blankets. He shouldn't be surprised at the hospitality because of the shack's use as a way station, but the volume of stores was unexpected.

He bent and rummaged through the metal cans. With a grin, he read one of the labels out loud. "U.S. Army Field Ration, B Unit. Apparently, we're not the first Americans to frequent this fine establishment."

Emily gigged and held out her hand. "What delicious cuisine is on the menu?"

"This can holds biscuits, something called confection, sugar, and coffee."

She wrinkled her nose. "Anything else?"

"Aha." He held up another can. "Much better. There are some M-units here. We can choose from meat stew with beans, meat stew with vegetables, or meat with vegetable hash."

"Tough choice. I guess I'll take the stew with vegetables."

He nodded and tossed her the container. "Sorry. No spoons."

"That's the least of our worries. Don't you think?"

"Definitely—"

Footsteps sounded outside, and Gerard yanked out his gun. He pushed Emily behind him and pointed the weapon at the door that swung open with a creak.

A slight man with receding hair stood on the threshold. He held up his hands in surrender. "*Je m'appelle* Fred, and I'm here to take you to my home where my wife will feed you. I will provide clothing, money, and train tickets. No questions asked. If you are in this hut, you are in need of saving."

Gerard gawked at Fred. "I'm—"

"Please, no names. It is better that way." He beckoned them to follow. "Come. You must be fatigued, but it is best to leave this place. My home is not far."

Emily groaned as she stood. "Please tell me there is a mattress in my future."

Fred nodded, his face beaming. "Yes, all the comforts you can imagine. You will stay the night as our guest. In the morning, we will take you to the station. We have tickets for the train to Bern where you can blend into the masses of the city, then make your way to your next destination."

"Okay." Gerard's heart constricted. A plan that would get them safely behind OSS walls and the end of their mission. The end of their marriage. He frowned and rubbed his chest. The annulment no longer held the allure it did at the beginning of this assignment. Mere months had passed since she walked into his classroom. How could she have gotten under his skin in such a short time?

She stopped, hands on her hips. "Are you coming?"

He tilted his head and grinned. "Impatient, aren't you?" Despite fatigue, hunger, and miles of travel, her porcelain skin glowed in the fading sunshine. More importantly, she was beautiful on the inside. An unshakeable faith in God, a sense of humor, and intelligence. Like no woman he'd ever met.

And he would never be the same.

---

Forty-eight hours later, Gerard and Emily sat in Allen Dulles's office debriefing the man who looked more like a professor than a spy in his tweed jacket and blue flannel slacks. His complexion ruddy, he had a small, graying mustache. Sharp blue eyes studied them from behind rimless glasses.

He sat back in the chair that squeaked with his every move. "You've told quite a tale. Lots of narrow misses, I'd say. I'm pleased you made it out alive. You've proven yourself capable. With the exception of going back into France, you can have your pick of assignments."

"Thank you, sir." Gerard ran a hand over his spiky hair. "I'm willing to serve wherever I'm needed most."

"I'm sorry I wasn't able to transmit more messages than I did...to be more helpful, sir." Emily rubbed the back of her neck.

"Nonsense. You were compromised early. It happens. You know the average life expectancy of a radio operator is six weeks. Needless to say, some last longer, but many perish almost immediately. You're lucky to be alive to tell the story...not that you can say anything to anyone, but you understand." Savory-smelling smoke from the pipe clenched in his teeth encircled his head.

Gerard swallowed a cough but resisted the urge to wave his hand to dispel the acrid cloud. Director Dulles wouldn't appreciate the action. "Yes, sir. Do you mind if I take a couple of days of R and R before making my decision. I'm sure Emily...uh...Agent Strealer could use the time as well."

"Absolutely. Report back to me in seventy-two hours. That enough time?"

"Yes, sir." Gerard executed a crisp salute.

"No need for that, son. We're not in the military here." He puffed on his pipe. "See the girl at the desk outside my office, and she'll show you to your quarters. They're not much, but they'll do in a pinch."

Gerard and Emily rose.

"By the way, you'll see a parade of people during your stay. My official title is Special Assistant to the American Minister, but it's Bern's worst-kept secret that I work in intelligence. Frankly, I like it that way. All kinds of individuals show up, probably hoping for favors in exchange for information. There seems to be a thriving guild of professional spies and traders of espionage who make the rounds in the city. The Germans, the British, and then finally me at night." He shrugged. "A tangled web of intrigue, to be sure."

"Thank you for everything, sir." Emily smiled, her face wan and etched with weariness.

"Thank you, young lady. Now, get some rest, and I'll speak to you again." Dulles pointed to Gerard. "A moment, Lucas?"

Gerard's mouth went dry. What had he done that one of America's chief spymasters needed to speak with him alone?

Emily looked at him, a furrow between her eyebrows, then slipped out of the room.

"Please be seated." Dulles motioned toward his recently vacated chair.

Dropping into the upholstered seat, Gerard swallowed in a desperate attempt to moisten his throat.

Dulles flipped open a folder in front of him. "I see from the mission file you and Agent Strealer acted as a married couple, then by your own report, the two of you wed for real while in France in order to get genuine papers. You've indicated a desire to have the marriage annulled which is certainly within my power to execute, but I sense some reticence in you." He removed his pipe and laid it in a chunky glass ashtray. He leaned across the desk, his keen blue eyes piercing Gerard's face. "My ability to read people is one of many reasons why I'm in this position. And I believe you've fallen in love with her, that you don't want an annulment."

"Well—"

"I'm not finished."

"Sorry, sir." Gerard wiped damp palms on his pants. He'd be more comfortable under a German interrogation than Director Dulles's examination of his feelings for Emily.

"You need to tell her, man. I see the way you look at her when you think she isn't paying attention. Unrequited love will gnaw at you. You must resolve this situation before we'll consider giving you another assignment. Understood?"

"Yes, sir."

"Terrified of the prospect, are you?"

Gerard bit back an embarrassed laugh. "More than a little, sir."

"Good." He chuckled. "Best get to it, then, son. She's put in for a transfer."

"Transfer?" Vaulting from the chair as if scalded, Gerard started to salute then dropped his arm. He hurried from the room, his mind racing. Why would she put in for a transfer? What department? Was she leaving OSS? Dulles was right; he needed to talk to Emily immediately. She seemed to care for him, but did her emotions run deeper than simple friendship? She responded to his kisses, but physical attraction doesn't make a relationship. Was it remotely possible that she loved him, or was she just good at pretending?

He skidded to a stop in front of the young woman at the desk outside Dulles's office. "Agent Strealer? Do you know where she went?"

The woman nodded and waved toward one of the hallways branching off the foyer. "Third door on the left."

"Thank you." Breathless, he trotted across the gleaming tile floor and into the corridor. One…two…three. The door was closed, and he lifted his hand to knock, then hesitated. What if she laughed in his face or unceremoniously threw him out for his audacity? He rubbed his forehead with cold fingers. No, she'd never act like that, but instead would let him down gently, somehow making her lack of feelings her fault.

Before he could chicken out, he knocked on the door.

Emily turned toward the sharp rap at the door. "Who is it?"

"Gerard." His voice was muffled.

Her heart leapt. He'd sought her out. "Just a minute." She finished folding the blouse she still held in her hands and laid it in the satchel parked on the bed. She hurried to the mirror and smoothed her hair, then pinched color into her cheeks. Her lips were dry and cracked, but cosmetics were not part of the kit she'd been given to replace the ragged clothing she'd worn all the way across France. She'd have to go without lipstick. Rolling her eyes at the image in the reflection, she shook her head. In the weeks during the escape, she'd looked much worse. Besides, what did it matter? She'd be gone within days anyway.

"Is everything okay, Emily?" Concern colored Gerard's words from behind the closed door.

A bittersweet smile curved her lips. He was still taking care of her. She pivoted away from her reflection. "Yes." She crossed the room and opened the door, drinking in the sight of his handsome face. "Sorry to keep you waiting."

"Director Dulles said you put in for a transfer."

"Yes, but why did he feel the need to share that with you?"

"He thought I'd want to know."

She raised an eyebrow. "Is he always so forthcoming with every agent's information?"

"No, maybe because we're married…" He grinned, but uncertainty clouded his eyes.

"Not for much longer." Her heart cracked at the thought, and she pinned a smile on her face. She couldn't exhibit how the knowledge pained her. "You'll go your way, and I'll go mine. Director Dulles indicated we could have plum assignments, and I've asked for Belgium. My knowledge of French should help, and if they agree, I'll learn Flemish before I go."

"By yourself? Are you sure?"

She cocked her head. "I'm surprised at you questioning my decision. I was unsure and immature when I started, allowing the criticisms and judgments of my family influence my thoughts and actions, but I've changed. This ordeal made me realize I am a strong woman, able to do things I didn't think were possible. I want to continue to grow and stretch. I've accepted that my family may never understand me, but I realize now they thought they had my best interests at heart."

His face pinked, and he shook his head. Embarrassment? A side of him she'd not experienced. He reached for her hands and cradled them in his larger ones. "I'm messing this up. I didn't mean to sound like I'm judging your choice." He cleared his throat. "What I'm trying to say is that I want to be your partner…for life…not just for the OSS. I don't want our marriage annulled. I love you and want you to remain my wife. I want to spend the rest of my life taking care of you." He grinned. "Even though you don't need assistance as you've told me so many times."

Emily stared at him, slack jawed. He loved her? He wanted to stay married?

"Say something, please." His smile faltered. "If you don't feel the same way, please let me down gently. Then I'll inform Director Dulles to go ahead with the paperwork dissolving our marriage."

With a soft touch, she ran a light finger along his jaw then smoothed out the frown that wrinkled his forehead. She raised up on her toes and touched her lips to his, their breath mingling. She pulled back a fraction and stared into his eyes. Could he feel her heart healing and swelling with his words? "I love you, too and would be honored to be your wife…well…keep being your wife."

Gerard pulled her into a fierce embrace then picked her up and swung her around. "Yes!" He put her down and showered her face with kisses. Her forehead. Her eyelids. Her cheeks. And finally, her lips. Tentative at first, the kiss deepened as the full force of their love became one.

THE END

## Historical Notes

I enjoy the opportunity to insert historical figures into my stories. *Spies & Sweethearts* features two real people who lived and served during WWII:

Allen Welsh Dulles (whose brother John Foster Dulles was Eisenhower's Secretary of State and the namesake of Dulles Airport in Virginia) graduated from Princeton University and immediately entered the diplomatic service. His first assignment was in Berlin, Germany, and he was transferred to Bern, Switzerland shortly before the beginning of World War I. He earned his law degree in 1926 and went on to become legal counsel to the delegations on arms limitations at the League of Nations. In October, 1941, Dulles was personally recruited by William Donovan for the Office of Strategic Services and stationed in Bern, Switzerland. He collected intelligence regarding German plans and activities.

Fred Reymond: Despite Switzerland's stance of official neutrality during WWII, many of her citizens were involved in fighting Nazi tyranny by smuggling weapons, gunpowder, ammunition, Jews, and downed pilots and aircrew. Fred Reymond was one of dozens of Swiss spies who passed information and people across the three foot high wall that runs the length of the Risoux Forest between France and Switzerland.

### What did you think of *Spies & Sweethearts?*

Thank you so much for purchasing *Spies & Sweethearts*. You could have selected any number of books to read, but you chose this book.

I hope it added encouragement and exhortation to your life. If so, it would be nice if you could share this book with your family and friends by posting to Facebook (www.facebook.com) and/or Twitter (www.twitter.com).

If you enjoyed this book and found some benefit in reading it, I'd appreciate it if you could take some time to post a review on Amazon, Goodreads, Kobo, GooglePlay, Apple Books, or other book review site of your choice. Your feedback and support will help me to improve my writing craft for future projects and make this book even better.

Thank you again for your purchase.


Blessings,

Linda Shenton Matchett

# Acknowledgments

Although writing a book is a solitary task, it is not a solitary journey. There have been many who have helped and encouraged me along the way.

My parents, Richard and Jean Shenton, who presented me with my first writing tablet and encouraged me to capture my imagination with words. Thanks, Mom and Dad!

Scribes212 – my ACFW online critique group: Valerie Goree, Marcia Lahti, and the late Loretta Boyett (passed on to Glory, but never forgotten). Without your input, my writing would not be nearly as effective.

Eva Marie Everson – my mentor/instructor with Christian Writers' Guild. You took a timid, untrained student and turned her into a writer. Many thanks!

SincNE, and the folks who coordinate the Crimebake Writing Conference. I have attended many writing conferences, but without a doubt, Crimebake is one of the best. The workshops, seminars, panels, critiques, and every tiny aspect are well-executed, professional, and educational.

Special thanks to Hank Phillippi Ryan, Halle Ephron, and Roberta Isleib for your encouragement and spot-on critiques of my work.

Thanks to my Book Brigade who provide information, encouragement, and support.

A heartfelt thank you to my brothers, Jack Shenton and Douglas Shenton, and my sister, Susan Shenton Greger for being enthusiastic cheerleaders during my writing journey. Your support means more than you'll know.

My husband, Wes, deserves special kudos for understanding my need to write. Thank you for creating my writing room – it's perfect, and I'm thankful for it every day. Thank you for your willingness to accept a house that's a bit cluttered, laundry that's not always done, and meals on the go. I love you.

And finally, to God be the glory. I thank Him for giving me the gift of writing and the inspiration to tell stories that shine the light on His goodness and mercy.

Read on for the first chapter in *The Mechanic and the MD*, book two in the "Sisters in Service" series.

*New Hampshire, June 1943*

## Chapter One

The factory's end-of-shift signal shrieked, piercing Doris Strealer's ears. She laid down the bucking bar then yanked off her red-and-white bandanna and finger-combed her brown hair. The only sister in the family with mousy brunette hair. Not russet-auburn like Emily's or corn-silk blonde like Cora's. She frowned. What did the color of her hair matter? It wasn't as if she was ever getting married. She had yet to meet a guy willing to date a tall gal, and at five foot eleven, she'd towered over every boy in high school and college. The workplace was proving no different.

Striding between the endless row of airplane wings, she walked to the time-clock station and slid her card into the machine's slot. The clock punched her card with a bang, and she returned it to its niche. She rotated her neck to ease the kinks in her shoulders. Gripping the metal bar for twelve hours a day while her partner Teresa attached thousands of rivets to airplane wings knotted her muscles like one of Grandma's homemade pretzels.

She stuffed the kerchief into her pocket and trudged to the women's locker room. Being one of America's Rosie the Riveters was nowhere near as glamorous as the magazine articles touted, but at least she wasn't stuck at a desk. She'd do almost any job to avoid holding a sedentary position.

"Want to go to the movies tonight, Doris?" Petite and pretty, Teresa had already exchanged her coveralls for a cute yellow polka-dot dress and white peep-toe shoes. "A bunch of us are going to meet up at the Majestic. The new Betty Grable musical *Coney Island* is playing. I'm sick to death of war movies, aren't you?"

"Maybe another time. It's my grandma's birthday today, and we're having a party for her."

"That sounds like fun."

Doris changed into her street clothes. "It's something to do. But the festivities won't be the same without Emily, who is overseas, and Cora is still mourning Brian's death even though it's been two years since he was killed during the Pearl Harbor attack. Not a very joyous atmosphere, but we give it a go."

"Yvonne says the war will be over by Christmas, then life can get back to normal."

"Even with the German army surrendering in Stalingrad in February and last month's victory in Tunisia, I don't think that's going to happen. The Allies have a long fight on their hands before Hitler gives up."

Teresa combed her raven-colored tresses. "Stalingrad. Tunisia. El Alamein. So many places I'd never heard of before this war started."

Doris cocked her head. "A lot has changed in the last eighteen months. Do you like your job, Teresa?"

"Well enough, I guess. Why? Don't you?"

"Not really. I'm proud to be doing something for the war effort, but I'm bored. Our work doesn't exactly require a lot of thought."

"Are you going to look for something else?" Teresa grabbed her pocketbook from inside the locker and slammed the door. She slipped her arm through the handbag's strap and headed toward the exit. "What else could you do?"

"I'd rather tinker with engines." Doris walked beside her partner. "Unfortunately, none of the garages in town will hire a female mechanic, and when I brought that issue up during my interview for this place, Mr. Meyer rolled his eyes. There must be somewhere I can work on cars or trucks."

They followed the crowd of women out of the building and walked across the street to the bus stop. Doris shielded her eyes from the pink-and-orange rays of the setting sun. "It's been over twenty years since women got the right to vote. Why don't we have the right to get the job that we want? It's not fair."

"No matter what job you secure, you're going to have to give it up when the men come home. Do you want to take a position you might love, only to lose it when the war is over?"

The six-fifteen bus shimmied and bucked as it rumbled toward them. Acrid diesel exhaust belched from the vehicle. Brakes squealed, and the lumbering beast came to a stop. Teresa coughed and waved her hand to dispel the fumes. "I like you, Doris, but I don't understand why you want to work on stinky engines." She climbed the stairs into the bus and deposited her coin in the box.

Doris followed her on board. "You may think it smells bad, but to me it's better than the scent of Evening in Paris." She sighed and dropped into the first vacant pair of seats. "Boyle Brothers and Mighty Mechanics are both hiring, but they're not accepting female applicants. They're going to be in a bind when the rest of the men are called up."

"Then you can swoop in to the rescue." Teresa grinned and sat next to her then leaned over and pointed out the window at a poster on the side of the bus stop shelter. "Or you can contact the Red Cross Motor Corps. They're looking for volunteers."

———————◆———————

Ron McCann bent over the patient lying on the operating table and began to remove the blood-encrusted bandage on the young soldier's leg. Thunder boomed and rain pounded the windows. The lights flickered but remained illuminated. For the time being. Deplorable conditions for an operating theater.

Sweat trickled down his spine despite the chill in the massive ballroom that once held dancing couples. One of thousands of centuries-old castles requisitioned by the British, Heritage Hall now served as a convalescent hospital. After a bombing in the north end of London by the Jerries, Heritage also acted as an overflow surgical center, today being the third time this week. He glanced across the mahogany-paneled expanse at the sea of wounded-filled gurneys. How many more young men waited in the corridors?

Piece by piece, he removed shrapnel from the boy's knees and shins then stitched the openings. Fortunately for the lad, the metal fragments had not done extensive damage. He might limp a bit but wouldn't lose either limb. On the downside, with such minor repairs required, the youngster would probably be back in combat within a matter of weeks.

Hours passed, and Ron continued to patch up American and British soldiers returning to merry old England from the lines. Most of his buddies from med school were assigned to various fronts, and he'd asked to serve nearer to the fighting, but the powers that be felt his skills were better used on English soil.

His eyes burned with fatigue, and his back screamed from hunching over the broken bodies of the boys who should be chasing girls in high school or pursuing their future in college. He was an old man in comparison. Fresh out of residency, he'd received his draft notice three months ago. A few weeks of army training, then a troop transport across the ocean, and a bumpy ride from Portsmouth to the crowded streets of Hemel Hempstead.

"This is the last patient, Dr. McCann." Sister Greene dabbed the perspiration from his forehead with a linen square clasped in a surgical clamp. He had no idea of the woman's age, but rumor had it she'd seen action during the Indian wars, the Mexican Revolution, and the Great War. Now in the twilight of her life, she was in the midst of armed conflict again. Her steely gaze and sharp tongue had sent more than a few junior cadet nurses crying into their pillows. Personality aside, she was a godsend in the operating room. Nothing caused her to flinch or faint.

"Thank you, Nurse. Another fine job. I appreciate your help." Ron snipped the last thread. He covered his work with a bandage and stepped back from the table. Two orderlies moved the patient to a gurney and wheeled him out the door to the dormitory-style ward.

"You should get some rest, Doctor."

"As should you." He smiled at the indefatigable woman. "But I'm guessing you plan something else for the remainder of the daylight hours."

A shrug lifted her shoulders. "There's inventory to be done, laundry that never ends, and as good as my staff is, I check their work to ensure the boys are getting the best possible care."

"Your work ethic and energy put me to shame, Sister Greene."

Pink tinged her cheeks, and she pressed her lips together. "Flattery will get you nowhere, Doctor."

He threw back his head and laughed, the sound echoing against the hard surfaces of the cavernous space. "Let me help you with inventory. Surgery always leaves me keyed up, so sleep is out of the question for the time being. I'd like to be of some use."

She studied him for a moment, then nodded. "Very well. I'll meet you in the dispensary. We'll begin there."

"Yes, ma'am." He touched his fingers to the side of his head in mock salute.

"You're not too old or too big for a paddling." She shook her index finger at him, but the twinkle in her eye belied her firm voice. "Ten minutes. Don't be late." She toddled through the door.

Ron removed his gloves, tossing them into an enamel bowl on the tray near the operating table, then untied the string the held the sterile gown over his uniform, dropping the soiled garment into the mesh bag propped against the wall. He walked to the sink and washed his hands, watching the orderlies and nurses clean the room and put it to rights for the next round of wounded.

He left the noise behind and hurried down the wide, gleaming staircase, its balusters individual works of art. The home's former ancestors glared at him from intricate, gilt frames, and he lifted a hand in greeting as he trotted past.

Sister Greene stood in front of a glass cabinet, holding a clipboard and wearing a deep frown.

"What is it?" He peered into the cabinet, and his eyes narrowed. The stock of pharmaceuticals, bandages, tape, and other consumables was minimal. "Did we use that much with this last influx of patients, or did the delivery fail to arrive again?"

"The latter, I'm afraid."

He raked his fingers through his hair and blew out a loud breath. "What is wrong with the army's system? We put in requisitions, and they fill them. How hard can that be?"

She opened her mouth to respond, but he held up a hand. "Strictly a rhetorical question, Nurse. I don't expect you to know the answer. Let's pray for a miracle and hope God sees fit to grant one."

Engines thrummed outside.

"If I'm not mistaken, more *visitors* just arrived." Ron frowned. "Inventory will have to wait."

"We'll be ready for you, Doctor."

"I'd expect nothing less, Sister." He flung the words over his shoulder as he raced from the room and headed to the foyer.

He pushed open the heavy front door. Outside, the raging maelstrom now simmered with a light mist and occasional thunder. A pair of ambulances parked on the gravel in front of the stone entrance. Each of the drivers held one end of a stretcher, and a hospital orderly gripped the other. They carted their loads inside. He pointed toward the ballroom, and they swept past him.

The lingering fragrance of flowers filled his nose, and he whipped his head toward the uniformed figures. Both women. With their hair stuffed underneath their tin hats, he hadn't noticed their gender. More and more of the drivers were female. What was Roosevelt thinking when he signed the order letting women into the armed forces?

Neville Thorson, a brilliant surgeon from London nudged his arm. "Your opinion is all over your face, and it's going to get you in trouble one of these days. Face it, Doctor. The gals are here to stay."

Ron shook his head. "They're to be protected and provided for, not assigned to war zones."

"Since when is England a combat zone?" Neville shoved his hands into his pockets.

"Hitler may not be bombing as regularly as he did in forty-one, but death remains a dangerous possibility every day."

"Get used to it, chap. Working side by side with the ladies is our reality." He grinned. "One for which I'm eternally grateful. Some of the drivers are real lookers."

"Women have no right in the Medical Corps, and I'm going to contact HQ about it. I don't want these women coming to my hospital."

Other Titles

## Romance

*Love's Harvest, Wartime Brides, Book 1*

*Love's Rescue, Wartime Brides, Book 2*

*Love's Belief, Wartime Brides, Book 3*

*Love's Allegiance, Wartime Brides, Book 4*

*Love Found in Sherwood Forest*

*A Love Not Forgotten*

*On the Rails*

*A Doctor in the House (The Hope of Christmas Collection)*

*Spies & Sweethearts, Sisters in Service, Book 1*

*The Mechanic & the MD, Sisters in Service, Book 2 (May, 2020)*

*The Widow & the War Correspondent, Sisters in Service, Book 3*

*(June, 2020)*

## Mystery

*Under Fire, Ruth Brown Mystery Series, Book 1*

*Under Ground, Ruth Brown Mystery Series, Book 2*

*Under Cover, Ruth Brown Mystery Series, Book 3*

*Murder of Convenience, Women of Courage, Book 1*

## Non-Fiction

*WWII Word Find, Volume 1*

**Linda Shenton Matchett** writes about ordinary people who did extraordinary things in days gone by. She is a volunteer docent and archivist at the Wright Museum of WWII and a trustee for her local public library. Born in Baltimore, Maryland, a stone's throw from Fort McHenry, she has lived in historical places most of her life. Now located in central New Hampshire, Linda's favorite activities include exploring historic sites and immersing herself in the imaginary worlds created by other authors.

Website/blog: http://www.LindaShentonMatchett.com

Facebook: http://www.facebook.com/LindaShentonMatchettAuthor

Pinterest: http://www.pinterest.com/lindasmatchett

Amazon: https://www.amazon.com/Linda-Shenton-Matchett/e/B01DNB54S0

Goodreads: http://www.goodreads.com/author_linda_matchett

Bookbub: http://www.bookbub.com/authors/linda-shenton-matchett

CPSIA information can be obtained
at www.ICGtesting.com
Printed in the USA
LVHW031001100121
676041LV00005B/403